BOBBY ON THE RUN

BOBBY

ON THE

RUN

Winston Bugle

Matador
5 Weir Road
Kibworth Beauchamp
Leicester LE8 0LQ, UK
Tel: (+44) 116 279 2277
Email: books@troubador.co.uk
Web: www.troubador.co.uk/matador

ISBN 978 1848764316

British Library Cataloguing in Publication Data.
A catalogue record for this book is available from the British Library.

All characters in this book are fictitious. Any resemblance to actual persons,
living or dead, is purely coincidental.

Typeset in 12pt Sabon by Troubador Publishing Ltd, Leicester, UK
Printed in the UK by

Matador is an imprint of Troubador Publishing Ltd

Printed in Great Britain by the MPG Books Group, Bodmin and King's Lynn

This book is dedicated to the lost faun in the forest drinking in the stream being watched and protected by the stoat

… And also to every police officer and their family members whose lives have been affected by unnecessary or malicious investigation by their employer.

Acknowledgements

I would like to thank the following people ...

My biggest thanks and love are to my 'Steb' and our children. 'Steb', in spite of everything you have maintained your faith in me and never given up despite me not being there for you as I really should have been. I know how much you have been through and I know your strength has been tested to the limit. I promise from now on, things are going to get much better. I love you so much. Thank you for giving me the best things life can give. Our children – you are too young to read this but I hope when you are old enough you will enjoy it and will give you the confidence that even the most dire situations can be overcome. It would not have been possible to write this without the love and inspiration all three of you have provided. My lovely family.

Dad, you have been very supportive for this project and have also been a key BOTR project member. Thank you for the help.

Simon Templar – many thanks for the feedback and support.

Mum, I know you're watching all this and I hope you feel I have dealt with things the right way. I miss you.

David Savannah. I consider myself very lucky to have this man on board to write the foreword. David is a Technical Consultant and retired police officer. David has extensive experience in dealing with Professional Standards Departments across the country and is one of the countries leading experts and authorities in his field. Thanks Dave!

Foreword

The deposed businessman Robert Maxwell, the disgraced senior police officer Ali Dizaei, and other prolific persons who have come to public notice are prime examples of bullies who because of their apparent power either financially or positional have used such privileges illegally and inappropriately. These are the ones that make the headlines; but what about the ones that don't, but still make the lives of others unbearable, stressful and in some cases futile.

The British Police Service is full of individuals wanting to better themselves by fair means or foul. The next rank, a bigger pension, a better job within the organisation, or an unnecessary course or travel excursion are all within the grasp of some who will stop at nothing to get what they want and do not care who or what they step over to do so. A bending of the rules and in some cases complete dismissal of the rules knows no bounds for the underhand methods that such persons will employ.

When it comes to criminal and or discipline matters however the Professional Standards Department does not always exude its principle level "Professional". Although there are many departments that are impartial in their investigations and employ innovative and talented investigators, there are many who simply fall short of the mark and are woefully "Unprofessional". On the receiving end of this is the police officer, who like any member of the public should be treated as innocent until proven guilty. Unfortunately all too often in my experience, the process is fraught with conjecture, poor management and sometimes false evidence being put to the officer from the same colleagues that will have a hand in deciding the officers fate.

This book although fictional but based on true life experiences overcomes the silence and denial by which some PSD departments thrive. Read it and decide for yourselves whether what goes on behind closed doors could be happening in your local police service.

David Savannah
Consultant

Preface

I am, at the time of writing this, a serving police officer.

Although this is a work of complete fiction, I write this story through my own experiences of police Professional Standards Departments and how they treat good hard working police officers who deserve to be treated better. I also thought it would be fun to write an outrageous fiction story myself.

Before I begin this story it is important that I explain who PSD are in relation to the Police Service…

PSD stands for Professional Standards Department. Every different police constabulary and force has their own PSD and their role is to police the police.

Police officers obviously have a great deal of responsibility and the general public have to be able to have complete faith that the police officers they entrust with the detection and prevention of crime and the protection of the lives and property of themselves, their family and friends are performing their role effectively, intelligently, honestly and within the laws of the land.

So for this reason it would seem that PSD departments are an essential part of the police and indeed, there are some police officers that do wrong and should not be in the role – unfortunately a large number of those sorts of people seem to work as officers in the PSD.

This is why a lot of frontline police officers, especially officers who have suffered at the hands of PSD investigations often refer to the Professional Standards Department as the *Double* Standards Department.

It seems police officers that apply to join the PSD are not really interested in dealing with criminals; they are not really interested in justice either. All it seems they are interested in is furthering their own careers without care or thought for whose toes they tread on to do so. All they seem to want to do is go through the ranks and it seems that they do not care if it is at the cost of real police officers careers who want to do what police should do: deal with criminals.

One of today's biggest problems with the police in the eyes of the public is that there are just not enough police officers on the streets. Whilst a great deal of this is down to lack of funding and too much stupid admin work for officers to complete, please also bear in mind that PSD officers will extremely rarely deal with real criminals in that role. They won't patrol the streets and keep you safe – they seem to spend most of their time twisting facts around and encouraging false evidence and lies from criminals who make complaints about good, decent police officers who do an effective job. Often these officers will end up with criminal convictions which may be (and often are) overturned on appeal cases. Sometimes the officers will get sacked, sometimes they go back to their jobs, sometimes they are so aggrieved and have had their lives ruined so much by PSD that they will leave anyway and give a more deserving employer their hard work. A lot of officers who previously were happy people end up having nervous breakdowns and suffering major depression. Their lives are completely destroyed.

I believe that there is very little public knowledge of how "police investigate the police" and the politics and personal selfish career aspirations of some of those that do so.

I do not condone police officers doing things that are wrong and against the nature of the job they have signed up for. I do believe that for officers that fall into this bracket they should be brought to justice and indeed, PSD departments have done some good work in this area.

However, I also do not condone malicious PSD investigations on police officers who are just trying to do their job under sometimes immensely difficult conditions, many of whom are completely innocent and that lead to their lives being ruined in order that a small number of people who have joined the police can tick the right boxes to further their own career prospects.

The PSD will support the people who burgle your homes, rob and beat up your sons and daughters, deal drugs etc to convict decent police officers trying to do the right thing. It is a disgraceful situation.

What follows in this book is a fiction story about a police officer under investigation by his PSD department from a fictional police force called Wessex Constabulary. The story is complete fiction and as far as I know PSD have never stooped to depths as low as are detailed in this story. The story however, reflects real feelings and emotions that police officers and their families go through during and after malicious PSD investigations on them.

I must stress, this is a story of fiction and in no way intended to cause any defamation to any police department. There are good and bad people in any job and in any department.

Prologue

I am Jack Lucas.

I was born in the early 1970s in mid Wales. My dad was in the Army serving in the Special Air Service. I rarely saw him due to this as he was often away working and he could never talk about most the things he did but despite this, he would give me some occasional juicy stories about his work. I loved these stories and felt very proud of my dad serving the country. I considered him a very brave and good man. My mum gave up work when I was born to look after me and my brother Max who was born two years later.

We lived in a large farm house on the outskirts of Hereford which my family inherited from my grandpa – my dad's dad who also served our country in the Second World War flying Lancaster bombers deep into German territory to "bomb the Hun and hit them in the goolies where it hurts." Grandpa used to furnish me with lots of war stories including how he and his crew escaped after being shot down over the Reichstag itself in Berlin. One of his crew was from a German family and spoke fluent German, so he bluffed their way through all the check points after the seven of them managed somehow to ambush a German anti aircraft crew and steal their uniforms (Grandpa joked that it was the same triple A crew that shot them down so they were asking for it). They took a vehicle and managed to escape Berlin and were picked up by a British Army unit working behind the enemy lines in France. They were nearly shot by them until my Grandpa shouted "Friend not foe" in a very English accent. It turned out that the Sergeant of the Army unit was a man called Reg who was serving in the same British Army unit that my dad later joined, the SAS.

Reg and Grandpa became good friends after the war and it was Reg's SAS stories that led my dad to join the Army and eventually join the elite unit.

I was very proud of my dad and grandpa serving the country with such bravery. I was very patriotic and hoped to live up to their standards. It was men like my dad and grandpa that won the war and kept the Great in Great Britain.

My dad eventually retired from the Army and got himself a job as a security consultant in the South of England. My mum didn't really want to move but it was such a well paid job and mum was just happy to have dad coming home from work each day rather than him being away for months on end.

So we moved to the County of Wessex when I was 15 years old.

I made friends easily in Wessex and quickly established a wide circle of friends. I began learning martial arts as my main hobby and entered and won several semi and full contact tournaments. This martial arts training I was to carry on throughout my life as a means of staying fit and healthy. I left school with an average education then went to college and got myself further educated with a BTec National Diploma in business and finance. I did not go to university – I kick myself now for it though as I would loved to have used my brain and got myself properly qualified and educated. What stopped me was my short term ambition which I was too impatient to wait any longer to fulfil, I wanted to save up for and buy a classic Lotus Elan sports car that I had always dreamt of. I considered that going to university would keep me from realising this dream to later than I wanted and I therefore wanted to just go straight out to work.

I got myself my first job as a car salesman and sold as many cars as I could. I discovered a natural talent for selling and within 6 months, aided by the cheap living costs at home with mum and dad, I had my Lotus Elan and I was a very happy twenty year old boy. How I didn't kill myself in that car I don't know.

Having discovered a natural talent for selling I then moved on into the world of corporate IT sales to big blue chip companies. I did very well for myself and through this was able to spend more money on fast cars and bought my first house.

After a few years of this I got bored. I wanted out of the sales world; I wanted to do something different. I wanted something more exciting and I wanted to do a job that would be of benefit to society, the community and to people in general. I had been brought up with good morals and to support people and I had a very firm idea of good and bad. I considered myself one of life's good people. I was a 'goody'. I didn't much like 'baddies'.

I decided to apply to join the Police. It was less money than I was currently earning at that time but I was fed up with my lifestyle and money was not such a driving factor for me anymore. The idea of being a police officer was exciting and seemed like a really good new fresh challenge for the next chapter of my life.

I was invited to the local constabulary's training headquarters to a selection day. I passed. This was followed by a further day in which as well as physical fitness tests, (which were far too easy, lots of very unfit people got in that should not have done) we had to do a presentation and assessed group activities. I passed and was offered a position as a Probationary Police Constable in the busiest city on the south coast, Southmouth.

I accepted the position, handed in my resignation to my

current employer and then after a nice little break of a couple of months, began my police training at the Ashford Police Training Centre in Kent. I passed all my exams and completed this initial training.

Now armed with warrant card I had become PC 1974 Jack Lucas.

I was stationed at my designated city police station on the south coast and sailed through my two year probation period with ease. I loved the job. I was gaining new skills all the time and I was seeing a side of life and people that most normal people would never get to see (although I now see that they are blessed to be generally sheltered from these sorts of people). I had built a reputation at work as a good officer to work with that could be relied upon in any situation to do the right thing. I had built a reputation which was feared by the local criminals as they knew that if I was on duty I would probably catch them at whatever illegal or nasty things they were doing that day or night. Everyone knew of PC Lucas.

Following completion of my probationary period I received three commendations over the next two years from the Chief Constable. One was for bravery whilst arresting a drink driver I caught off duty whose reply to caution was made by crunching up his hand into a fist and swinging it at me necessitating a high level of force from myself to incapacitate and restrain him until uniformed and equipped units arrived to take him away. The other two were for acts of bravery whilst at work including my arrest of a man who shot a gun in my direction!

Everything was going great. The money was awful but I knew how much it would be before I joined. I loved the job. I loved the excitement each new shift on duty would bring and most of all, I loved locking up criminals – It was my personal challenge to try and arrest more criminals than anyone else in the station. Drug dealers, drink drivers, the Saturday night idiots, robbers, burglars, lunatics on the loose, you name them, I nicked them. I got occasional complaints from people but I never worried about them – I could always justify my actions and at the end of the day, people don't like being arrested. The complaints were normally from drunken idiots who did not know how to behave and always tried to fight when under arrest.

On top of my job going very well I also met the love of my life, Louise. We fell in love instantly. We planned a family and had a lovely daughter, Mollie. Soon afterwards Louise was pregnant again with our son, Jenson. Life was really going well. I was now a very proud partner and father – my family became my life and Louise and I planned to marry.

Then one day it all changed for me. This is the story of what happened and how twisted the police organisation can be ….

1

Another Saturday night

Saturday 4th August 2007 2200 hours

So far it was a run of the mill duty on a Saturday night in Southmouth. I was standing outside the Bridewell (custody suite) at the station with Steve who I was paired up with for the night. Tonight there were lots of people drinking in the various pubs, bars and clubs of the city. Before the night was over I knew that I would probably have arrested at least two people for public disorder / drunken offences. I had already nicked a large Polish man that door staff of a pub opposite the station had ejected. When I intervened he shouted in a heavy drunken Polish accent, "Fuck the Police, I kill the Police" and lashed out with a heavy kick that connected with my thigh. Assisted by the door staff and my colleague Steve, we quickly took him to the floor and handcuffed him to the rear. Still struggling, it wasn't easy walking an 18 stone bloke fighting along the way to the rear of the waiting police van, trying to sit down to prevent us from walking him and still lashing out with his feet.

My thigh really hurt. I doubted I would get anything in the way of compensation for the assault on me. Even though I arrested him for Assaulting a police officer and I had witnesses and CCTV evidence of the assault I know that the courts care little for the welfare of police officers carrying out their duty. I was also hot. It was a warm night and the body armour we have to wear was sucking out sweat like a leach sucking blood. On top of that, because our role on a Saturday night was high visibility policing to try and deter violent crime I had to wear my high visibility jacket, utility belt with all my personal protection equipment on it including hand cuffs, CS spray, retractable baton etc and my Custodian, which is the traditional cone shaped hat of the British Bobby.

Steve and I were still trying to calm down after having to fight and restrain the Polish bloke all the way to his cell where we pinned him down and searched him to ensure he had nothing with which to harm himself or more importantly, us. We then had to perform a split second "cell exit" procedure where the last Officer in the cell has both the prisoners hands in a wrist lock whilst the prisoner is face down on the floor (this kind of looks like someone holding a wheel barrow up on its wheel), other officers then leave the cell leaving one holding onto the last officers belt. When it is safe, the officer holding the last officers belt hauls him out of the cell so the prisoner has no time to get back up and run at us before the door is shut. Steve was the last officer on this occasion and it was me that hauled him out at his command.

As usual, once the door was slammed shut there was a cacophony of banging and swearing the other side of the cell door which trailed off as we all walked away wiping the sweat from our foreheads.

"Cup of tea?" said Matt the custody Sergeant as he walked into the custody kitchen. Unusually for a custody Sergeant, Matt was chilled out and friendly and had no big ideas over and above his station like some do.

"No thanks," I replied. "Got a bit to do and I need to write my pocket note book up for this."

Everything you do goes in your PNB (pocket note book), especially when you use force to restrain someone and the reasons why you did. Your PNB can be used in court as evidence and it is your first account of everything. I needed to get the full details of his assault on me in the book and what I did from that point on. I thought it unlikely that this male would complain about me but you never know. You have to cover your arse in the police like you just would not believe.

After we had written up our PNB's we went out on foot again to patrol the streets. "Jesus Jack, he put up quite a fight didn't he" said Steve. Steve was the most experienced member of my shift with 16 years of service and was a highly respected area car driver in the station. He had the highest arrest figures in the station and was well known for his no nonsense practical approach to policing.

"Reckon he was on more than just alcohol," I replied. Steve nodded his agreement.

We walked up past the civic centre and its high clock tower towards one of the city's parks. The parks were dark places ideal for hiding the local scrotes who liked to rob unwary lonely drunk people as easy prey for a beating and taking their wallet, mobile phone or anything else of value they had. We had a recent spree of robberies on Saturday nights at this time in the parks. Steve and I were determined to catch them at it or at least put them off with our presence. I always joked to Steve that his presence was enough to put anyone off coming into the city full stop. He took the digs well and he gave back as good as I gave him. What we really liked doing at night in the parks was to wear dark clothing so we could hide in the shadows and catch out the criminals. Unfortunately tonight because of the stipulations of uniform for high visibility public order patrol we stood out like big green and yellow bogies on the Queens Royal handkerchief. At least we were a deterrent I supposed but not nearly as much fun as skulking around in the shadows and catching them red handed.

We hadn't been walking through the park long when we heard a distant shout of distress and then another two voices that sounded like two young males doing an impression of a Jamaican gang member – they were the distinct voices of members of the local gang, the local robbers and burglars. The local scrotes…

We rounded the corner and I could clearly see, some 100 yards from our position, a small group of what looked like 5 young males typically wearing hooded tops surrounding another male who looked unsteady on his feet and dressed in a shirt and jeans, probably on his way back from a night venue. One of the hooded males was prancing around in front of the shirted male waving something in his direction. There was a glint of metal. A knife. Another hooded male pushed the male with the shirt and he fell over.

No time to waste. They hadn't seen us yet.

I immediately pressed the transmit pressle on my personal radio, "Charlie Papa One Two (our designated call sign for the night, CP12) to Control, Urgent…"

The control room responded, "Control, go ahead Charlie Papa One Two…"

"Location Main City Park. Robbery in progress. 5 males attacking another. Attackers are armed with at least one knife. Urgent back up to assist. We are dealing now."

I then switched my mind off from the radio as my adrenaline surged with the knowledge of what I now had to do. I sprinted the distance to the group, Steve was behind me but I could hear him and knew he was right with me. I didn't want to give the offenders a chance to escape so I didn't shout "Police! Stop!" as you see them do on television. Instead, as I closed the gap I focused on the male with the knife in his hand. He was just turning and had noticed me but I was running fast. I was carrying a lot of momentum and even though I'm not a big man, I'm heavily built for my size. I stuck my head down. I grabbed him round the waist with my right arm. My head was under the hand he was carrying the knife with and I gripped his knife hand with my left hand. The momentum took us both heavily to the ground with a thud and I could hear the air expel from his lungs as he was winded on the ground. My left hand was still controlling his knife hand and I quickly brought my right hand there too. With this I then twisted his hand into a wrist lock.

I shouted "Drop the knife!"

He refused. I put some more pressure on his wrist twisting it some more. He screamed in pain and the knife clattered to the floor. With knife man under control I kicked the knife away from the melee and looked around to see where Steve had got to.

I could see Steve running after the other four males who

were trying to get away. I couldn't see the shirt wearing male anywhere. He was gone. It was just me and knife male now. I turned around to face him to tell him he was under arrest for Attempt Robbery and Possession of an Offensive Weapon but as I did so my grip on his hand and wrist slipped. He suddenly put his hand down to his left sock and pulled out another knife. With this he swiped wildly in my direction. I jumped back and the knife just missed my left thigh which could easily have severed the artery there if it had cut me. I didn't have time to reach for my CS spray or my tactical asp baton which I would have to draw and then extend. Instead my hands naturally came up into a protective guard which is probably the worst thing to do when faced with a knife as you are opening up your hands and arms to be cut too. But I was acting on instinct now. The male then made a roaring noise and lunged at me again with his knife. I jumped back again. His hood came down. I did not recognise him. This was unusual as I knew all the local scrotes and they knew me. Knife male swiped at me again, and again I side stepped avoiding the arc of the knife. It was clear to me now that he wasn't messing around. He seemed to be intent on killing me rather than escaping! As he missed on the last swipe it was also quite clear to me that I had to decisively put knife male out of action. I wasn't going to die tonight. I aimed a powerful right cross straight into his chin with all my power. The chin is known in boxing slang as the knockout button, (it sends a shockwave through the jaw to the brain) and knock him out the punch did…. Crack! I could feel his jaw go loose and heard his teeth crack together as he just dropped to the floor as if he was a puppet that just had the strings holding him up cut off. This was not an excessive amount of force in the circumstances. The male was trying to attack me with a knife. I could have been killed. I would have been justified in drawing my asp baton and hitting him full power on the head using deadly force. Police have extensive training on use of force and are trained in something called the Conflict Management Model which specifies levels of force available to use in specific circumstances – this level of force was well within that training and it was also well within the legislation, Section 117 of PACE (Police And Criminal Evidence Act) that dictates the level of force police may use in arresting offenders. It was also well within the law that dictates the level of force any person, police or not may use to defend themselves.

I had nothing to worry about although I was concerned that I didn't want him to have an injury like a broken jaw – I know how difficult life can be made by PSD for officers in the aftermath of such events. My over riding feeling though was elation at still being alive and not bleeding to death in a dark park alone.

I bent down over the now unconscious knife male and checked his vital signs – he was breathing and his pulse felt good. He was beginning to stir and wake up. He was bleeding from his mouth. I quickly turned him over and applied my hand cuffs to this unpredictable violent male. Once the cuffs were on I began searching him.

"What the fuck are you doing you nonce" he said. As he said this I found some white pills in his front trouser pocket.

I replied to him, "I'll tell you what I'm doing, I'm nicking you. You are under arrest for Attempt Robbery, Possession of an Offensive Weapon, Assault Police and …" at this point I held up his white pills which were in a plastic deal bag so he could see them, "…on suspicion of Possession of a Class A drug. To this you do not have to say anything but it may harm your defence if you do not mention when questioned something you later rely on in court. Anything you do say may be given in evidence" – this is the caution which must be read to the suspect at the earliest practical opportunity on arrest. The next bit I had to say is the reason for his arrest – "Your arrest is necessary for the prompt and effective investigation of the offences and also to preserve evidence and you are a danger to the public." Knife male replied, "Suck your mum!" I have never known quite what scrotes mean by this but it is a common phrase in their 'gangster language'.

"What's your name?" I said to him.

"Fuck you" he replied and spat at me.

The spit missed but this was now a great worry. A lot of people police have to deal with (especially drug users) have infectious blood diseases such as hepatitis and HIV etc. There was blood in his spit due to the blow he had taken from me. Hepatitis or HIV can ruin your health forever. I turned him round and held him to the ground in a position that he could not spit at me again.

It was only now that I was becoming aware of the radio attached to my jacket. I could hear the control room saying urgently, "Control to Charlie Papa One Two, please come in. Are you in order?" over and over. I heard Steve's voice, "Charlie Papa One Two, we got split; PC Lucas is still in the park. I am state 9 with two males and need a van. I'm in order. Please welfare check on PC Lucas." State 9 is the force code to mean that he had arrested the two males.

Before the control room could come back on I transmitted, "PC Lucas to Control. I'm still in the park. I'm State 9 also. I too need a van and two knife tubes please. I'm in order but my subject is very violent."

I could hear a siren and see blue strobe lights through the trees bordering the edge of the park. It was one of the station's public order vans and it drove through a gap in the trees and into the park. The van drove up to my position and the occupants got out. Out of the van came my Sergeant, Lee, a good bloke and the best skipper I have ever worked with, two of the other guys on my shift who were brand new probationers and Inspector Mann. The latter officer filled me with dread. Inspector Mann was not a liked Inspector. He was out of touch with the officers on the ground and was a real yes man to his seniors. He just wanted to look good and was the sort of person who wouldn't hesitate to step on others' toes to climb the promotion ladder. In fact the most recent rumour was that he was about to start a job in PSD to secure his promotion to Chief Inspector. Not the sort you want to work with. "Where's your hat?" said Inspector Mann.

"Funnily enough sir it fell off when this bloke was trying to kill me." Did he detect the sarcasm? I doubted it.

"What's happened to his face Jack?"

My prisoner piped up, "He fucking punched me!"

"Did you?" said Inspector Mann to me raising an eye brow.

"Yes I punched him as hard as I bloody could sir he was attacking me with a knife!"

At this point Inspector Mann directed the two new PC's on my shift to pick the prisoner up and place him in the van. He walked past me and said, "We need to talk back at the station Jack."

My skipper Lee came up to me and said quietly, "Sorry it took us so long Jack, that twat Mann told me to wait for him to get his gear on to join us. I would have got here sooner. Good work though Jack! Are you ok?"

"Yeah I'm ok Sarge. Bit of a hectic night isn't it. Why does the Inspector want to speak to me back at the station?"

"Dunno, you know what he's like though" said Lee as he rolled his eyes, "good collar though mate."

2

Directed duties

Sunday 5th August 2007 0345 hours

It transpired that my prisoner was an extremely well known violent nominal from the London area named Mitchell Connor. He was wanted for several offences of robbery, burglary and failing to attend court. This meant that he was remanded in custody and I had to put a file together documenting evidence in relation to tonight's incident. This meant extensive note book entries, a long detailed statement from myself and Steve and several form filling and because he was being remanded in custody, everything had to be copied and put in three separate files. One for the CPS (Crown Prosecution Service); one for the defence but with any sensitive information omitted and one for our local Criminal Justice Unit. It's a lot of work that takes hours so that was myself and Steve grounded for the night in the station buried under a mountain of paper work.

Steve also had to do files for the other two he had arrested so I wanted to help him. They were local well known scrotes and were denying any involvement with Connor.

Only God knew where the aggrieved party, the male wearing the shirt had got to. That was a mystery which was a real shame as his evidence would have been key to an effective prosecution on Connor.

It is hard work doing this amount of paper work in the early hours of the morning after having to fight and restrain people when you would be tired anyway even if you had done no work so it takes a lot of concentration to make sure you have completed all the numerous forms and not missed anything.

I told Steve we needed to do a handover file for the next shift to take over for the Polish bloke from earlier as he was in drink (drunk) still and wouldn't be fit for interview until tomorrow. I was half way through my arrest statement when Inspector Mann walked into the report writing room (the room that officers do their paper work in).

He looked annoyed and said, "Jack, I thought I told you to come and see me when you got in."

"Yes sir, sorry. It's just my prisoner is being remanded and I need to make sure that I get all the file done before I go off duty. I was going to come and find you after that" I replied.

"Well Jack, come to my office now. We need to have a serious talk." I was nervous, I had done nothing wrong but that didn't mean that Inspector Mann wouldn't find something to criticise me about.

We walked into the duty Inspector's office and Mann closed the door behind us. We both sat down. I didn't wait to be invited. Whilst I respect rank I'm not that subservient to middle management, especially not the likes of Mann.

"Jack," began Inspector Mann "I have just come off the phone to PSD. They are not happy with your last arrest. They have instructed me to take you off frontline duties with immediate effect."

I was dumbfounded. "What?!" I replied, "Why? I didn't do anything wrong. The guy was trying to cut me with a knife for Gods sake."

"Jack, you knocked half his teeth out and rendered him unconscious" said Mann.

"Well he's lucky his jaw isn't broken and I'm even luckier to be alive. Can't you see I did nothing wrong?"

"Well," said Mann, "that's for PSD to decide. In the meantime you are grounded in the station with immediate effect and are not to go out on frontline duties until further notice."

I felt like a golden eagle that had just had its wings clipped off. I didn't join the police to be an office monkey or an admin assistant. I joined to fight crime. What was more, I had done nothing wrong. Had I acted differently I may still be lying in a pool of my own congealing blood with no life left in me. Not fair. Inspector Mann then added, "PSD are also concerned that you have two other outstanding complaints that they are investigating."

Yes I did have two other complaints but they were nothing to worry about, just drunken yobs making malicious complaints because I arrested them. All my actions in both cases were justified and I had no worries about the complaints. It suddenly dawned on me that PSD were reacting very quickly to a complaint and I didn't think Connor was making any complaint. The custody Sergeant would have told me if he was.

"Sir, how were PSD made aware of this?" I asked.

Mann responded curtly, "I told them. It was the right thing to do."

I knew Mann was a prat but this really took the biscuit. He must have been able to see the anger in my face as I said between gritted teeth, "What exactly did you tell them sir?"

Mann said, "I told them you punched your prisoner.

Why didn't you use your verbal skills and voice commands?"

I was gob smacked. What planet was Mann on? I couldn't contain any pretence of respect for the man anymore. "What? He was trying to kill me you twat! I also understand that back up was delayed getting to me because you wanted to stick your big fat nose in. That could have cost me my life and my family a partner and father! You are the one that should be taken off frontline duties but then I suspect that you have forgotten what it's like to work the streets anyway."

I was shouting at him by now. He looked white faced and surprised that I should talk to him like this but he was asking for it. I was stressed out and angry. I then said, "I'm going home now. I'm too stressed to stay here." I stormed out of his office.

I found Steve and told him that something bad had happened and that I couldn't stay. Steve told me it was all right and he would finish my file for me. I think he could see how stressed I was. Steve asked what the matter was but I told him I would tell him later. Right now I was struggling to come to terms with my meeting with Inspector Mann.

I phoned Louise to tell her what happened. She was gutted for me. She knew how proud I was of what I did and how much my job meant to me. I told her I was coming home and she sounded really worried about it all. I told her not to worry and that I was coming home right now. I didn't want Louise to worry. It felt like my career was over. At least I still had my family.

3

Stress

I came straight home from the station on Sunday morning. Louise was waiting for me at the front door as I pulled up in my car on the drive. I got out of the car and Louise held her arms open to hug me. I grabbed Louise and we hugged. I was trying hard not to let my feelings show but I couldn't help it. Maybe it was post traumatic stress I don't know but having someone try and kill you, surviving it and then being punished for acting appropriately in the circumstances and apprehending the offender who was not safe to be at large in public, I was feeling so emotional. The moment Louise embraced me I broke down in tears. Louise took me to bed and we spoke about the events that night. Later I went to sleep.

Monday was due to be one of my days off anyway which was just as well because I was still not ready to return to work. Louise took the day off work and we went for a walk and had a picnic to try and chill out. We tried to take our minds off things by discussing where and when we would next go on holiday. Holidays were one thing that we all looked forward to so much but it was hard at that moment to think of much else apart from last night. It was a nice day but everything was over shadowed by my situation at work. It was the last thing Louise needed. She was 6 months pregnant now and I had to be giving her a peaceful life. She shouldn't be feeling stressed out with my ridiculous work situation. She told me that I should have a medal for the arrest not be punished. I tried to explain to her how evil PSD can be in these situations but it's hard to explain to someone who is not involved in the police as the way they operate is just so over the top and totally disproportionate to real life.

I couldn't relax at all. I just kept replaying the events again and again in my head and considering if there was anything I could have done differently in the situation. Each time I concluded that what I did was absolutely right. There was no time to reach for my asp baton or my CS spray as I was busy trying to avoid the attacks. I executed my punch when I saw a split second opening. Had I not taken action at that precise moment, the knife may have caught me on the next swipe or lunge. I could have been dead or seriously injured. Better to be tried by twelve than carried by six as the saying goes. Still, it didn't make me feel much better.

We went home after our time out. No sooner had I closed the front door when there was a loud knock at it. I stopped and turned around. The person knocking either ran down the drive or was hiding in the front bushes ... I saw no one anywhere near our house before I shut the door. I opened the door. I saw two people; one was a male in his late fifties. He had grey hair around the sides and back with nothing on top. He was quite round in shape and over weight. The other was a female aged perhaps in her late forties with greying hair. Both were wearing suits.

The female spoke, "I am Inspector Burton of the Professional Standards Department."

She held up a warrant card that looked just like mine. She went on, "This is my colleague, Nick Link, he is my co worker."

I knew what that meant: He was a retired police officer working with PSD as a civilian assistant. Inspector Burtons 'bag man' in other words.

She continued, "Jack we are here today investigating your assault on Mitchell Connor on Saturday night. You are under arrest on suspicion of Assault Occasioning Grievous Bodily Harm. I need to advise you that you do not have to say anything but it may harm your defence if you do not mention when questioned something you later rely on in court. Anything you do say may be given in evidence."

I didn't know what to say. There was no need to arrest me; I would have happily attended a voluntary interview in relation to this. This was overkill and disproportionate.

I eventually replied, "Well in that case you had better get on the phone to my solicitor and my Federation Friend." I had a right to legal assistance in interview and I used the solicitor that had represented me in such interviews before although I had never been arrested before like this. My Federation Friend was a representative of the Police Federation. The Federation are like a union but they are not quite a union as police officers are not allowed such luxuries. The Federation have little power but can help with legal financial assistance and supposedly welfare support.

Louise rushed over, "What's going on Jack? Who are these people?" Louise eyed them suspiciously.

"It's the PSD Louise; I have to go with them now to be interviewed about Saturday night."

"They are arresting you?" said Louise.

I replied, "Yep. It will all be sorted out soon though." Little did I know what was to come …

4

Locked up

What was going on? They were not even ready to interview me straight away. So I had to sit in a cell in a police station I was not familiar with for what felt like hours. My watch and all my personal possessions had been taken from me when I was booked into the custody centre. Luckily it was a custody Sergeant I did not recognise that booked me in although it was still embarrassing being booked into custody as a police officer. Why was I waiting? My solicitor arrived immediately and I would have thought that PSD would have been ready to go straight into interview – surely the Professional Standards Department couldn't be that unprofessional and unprepared?

What was making things worse for me was that in the cell next door was a male of the 'No Fixed Abode' type. He was very loud and was shouting constantly, "Suck the shit from your mothers bum" again and again whilst banging on his cell door, he was clearly heavily in drink but what was worse was the smell from him. He had to have been one of the smelliest prisoners I have ever smelt and that was saying something.

It wasn't long before I heard someone opening his door to try and get him to quieten down, it was a males voice, "Look, would you please try and keep the noise d … Argh!" the person speaking to the prisoner didn't get to finish his sentence and screamed out loud in shock or pain, I wasn't sure which. I heard the cell door being slammed shut again with a loud bang.

I could hear the prisoner cackling a horrible laugh and saying, "That'll teach you, drink it! Drink it!" then I heard someone else running up to the door.

"You ok John, what's happened?"

I then heard what must have been John's voice, "Bloody Fletcher, I opened the door and he threw his fucking sperm at me."

I then heard the prisoners voice again, "Driiiiiink iiiiitt, drink it, drink it, drink it!" It was then I realised who my cell neighbour was; Kevin Fletcher. Fletcher was a notorious Southmouth heroin addict and one of the most disgusting people ever put on the planet. One of his favourite tricks was to masturbate in his cell and then when the door was opened he would flick his semen at police officers or detention officers. When he did this he would often say things like, "I've got Hep C and now you have it too." Often officers would enter his cell with riot helmets on and the visor pulled down. I actually knew of a custody Sergeant that got sacked after Fletcher had flicked semen on him, it landed on the custody Sergeant's lip and he just flipped and kicked Fletcher half to death in retribution. It is easy to say that he shouldn't have reacted like that and indeed, he should not have done but how would you feel if someone tried to deliberately infect you with hepatitis C and HIV? It's basically Attempt Murder.

Custody centres were often full of smelly prisoners though but it was rare that I had to be so close to someone so smelly for so long, I imagined my lungs were changing colour inside me he smelt so bad.

Hours still passed… My patience was very much wearing thin. Still, at least my new next door neighbour, Fletcher seemed to have shut up now. I pressed the button near the cell door to attract the attention of the custody staff.

A Detention Officer came to the door, "What's up?" he said.

"Mate, any chance I could have a chat with the custody Sergeant, I have been here hours now. I would have thought PSD would be ready to interview me immediately upon my arrival. What's going on?"

The DO replied, "Sorry mate I don't know. All I can tell

you is that the rest of the custody centre has been emptied of other prisoners. They have all been transferred to other custody centres, seems PSD are trying to keep this all hush hush, I'll get the skipper mate."

"Thanks" I replied. I was feeling very nervous now. There seemed to be a lot more going on than I was being told.

Seconds later the custody Sergeant appeared at my door, "Hello Jack, sorry to keep you in the dark but we have been instructed that way by PSD. We know no more than you do. It's been bedlam trying to get all the other prisoners out. Tell you what; I will leave the door open for you. I have heard about you, you have a good reputation. It's just you, me and John the DO in here at the moment ok. Your solicitor is waiting outside right now. As soon as we know more we will tell you but I am sorry to say that we have been instructed you are not to make any calls home or have any contact with the outside world at all at the moment."

Now I was very worried indeed. What on earth was going on?

I waited still longer for what felt like another five hours. I would have been bored stiff if I wasn't so worried. I couldn't stop thinking about Louise; she would have been calling to find out what was going on. What were they telling her? They weren't telling me anything at the moment. It was as I was thinking about this that I heard footsteps coming down the corridor towards my cell. Inspector Burton and Nick Link appeared at the cell door along with Inspector Mann. "For Gods sake, why is he here too?" I thought.

Inspector Burton then opened her mouth and said one of the most shocking things I have ever heard in my life, "Jack. You need to know that since we arrested you, Mitchell Connor died in his cell as a result of the injury he sustained whilst under arrest by you. As a result of this, I am further arresting you on suspicion of Manslaughter... "

Burton was still talking but her voice was fading into the back ground, I couldn't hear her or anything else. My ears started making a whining sound in my head, I felt dizzy and my vision blurred. I kept hearing Burtons words, "manslaughter" again and again in my head echoing, fading. Then everything went black. I lost consciousness.

5

The stitch up

Saturday 8th September 2007 1130 hours

I came to on a medical bed. I had an intravenous drip attached to my arm and a doctor was examining me whilst at the same time another man was taking a photograph of my right hand, the hand I struck Connor with. All of a sudden the memory of everything came back to me in a sudden rush. I felt pure dread. Had anyone told Louise what was happening yet? I was so scared I would not be able to see her and our kids except for prison visits for years now. What sort of life would that be for any of us?

The doctor began talking. He said, "Finally you are awake. I'm not sure exactly what happened to you but you lost consciousness last month and have been in a coma since that time. We suspect it was induced by shock. I wasn't expecting you to come out of the coma so soon."

A month?! "What has been going on? Where am I?"

The doctor replied, "I am Doctor Hudson. I am specially employed by Wessex Constabulary. You have been transferred from the police station to a special detention centre out of the county."

What did he mean 'special detention centre'? In my seven years of policing I had not heard of any such thing.

Dr Hudson continued, "I am to tell Inspector Burton when you are fit for interview. I will give you a day's rest and then, as long as there are no more complications I will certify you fit for a criminal interview."

All I cared about was Louise and the kids. "Does Louise know what is going on? Has anyone told her? Is she ok? She is pregnant you know."

Dr Hudson replied, "I am sorry, I know nothing about that. Maybe Inspector Burton can assist you when you see her."

Dr Hudson then left the room and I was on my own. I studied the room. It was very spartan. Apart from the trolley style bed I was lying on there was a plastic chair next to my bed, a small padlocked cabinet was on the far side of the room with a clock above it. There were no windows and set in the wall to the left of the bed was a metal door with no door handle.

I was allowed time to recuperate and food and drink

was brought to me during the day. I was feeling very agitated. I was extremely worried for Louise and the kids and I was confused about where I was. I couldn't sleep that night but by the sounds of things I had enough sleep over the last month.

By the next morning my solicitor came in escorted by two very heavily built looking men wearing black t-shirts and trousers.

"Mr Lucas. I don't know what's going on. I know they have arrested you for manslaughter to this Connor character but everything is very unusual. I don't know where we are here. All I know is I had to fly by helicopter and I was blindfolded until I was allowed in the building. It is most unusual indeed. I have seen Inspector Burton and she is going to give me disclosure in a minute. As soon as I have had this I will come back to you before we go into interview. Oh, and don't worry about Louise and Mollie. They are obviously upset but Louise's parents are looking after them. I have told Louise everything I can at this stage and have promised to do my best here for you all. I will be back in a bit."

With that, my solicitor went off with the two heavies following him. Who were they? They didn't look much like police officers to me, more like brainless thugs.

Exactly one hour later my solicitor returned to my room. The two heavies were with him.

"Please can you two gentlemen leave the room so I can speak with my client in privacy," my solicitor said.

The two heavies obliged and closed the door. They must have been waiting outside. My solicitor had a very bemused look on his face. "Very strange goings on indeed Mr Lucas. I will be upfront and honest with you. I may even give you unprofessional advice here that I would not expect you to take. But please listen to what I have to say …"

My solicitor went on with all the information Inspector Burton had disclosed to him. Connor had indeed died in custody. The basic belief was that he had died as a result of the blow I struck him with when he attacked me with the knife. Pretty basic and obvious really, that is what I would have concluded too as an officer investigating this. When there is a death in custody someone has to take the blame. The custody centre is shut down and an investigation takes place. What my solicitor also told me was that after he was given disclosure, Inspector Burton and Nick Link left the room but Link had accidentally left his open brief case under the desk. My solicitor noticed this and could see a file entitled: 'Mitchell Connor, DOB: 13/10/85 Post Mortem Report. Top secret.' This had not been disclosed to my solicitor but my solicitor was a shrewd fellow and a risk taker. Whilst the PSD personnel were out of the room he picked it up and looked at it. The contents were most interesting for according to the

Coroner, Mitchell Connor had not died as a result of any blow to his face or head. It turns out Connor had a condition in his heart that meant he could have died at any moment. It was this heart condition that was the cause of his death not my action in incapacitating him. There was also a minutes sheet attached to the front of this report that stated that another, edited report was to be created resting the blame of Connors death on me. Neither I nor my solicitor could understand why they were doing this. But they were. My solicitor told me that he was out of his depth and that there was some deeply disturbing injustice being created here. He told me that there was not one uniformed police officer in sight in the building. All the personnel seemed to be heavies like the ones he came in with. He seemed to think they were hired civilian security personnel.

His advice to me was that we would go ahead with the interview as normal. I would answer relevant questions and justify my use of force. We would then ask for a copy of the coroner's report before finishing the interview. The 'unprofessional advice' that he gave me was that I should seek any means to escape from the place and I should use any force available for me to do so. He explained to me that what was going on was unlawful and that I didn't have much to lose as in the face of the prosecution evidence and no witnesses to corroborate my story of Connors attack on me I would be facing a good many years locked up in jail. My solicitor told me that he would speak to some 'friends of his' and do whatever he could to assist me but that he couldn't make any promises.

So my mind was made up. I would do the interview, I would then make some attempt at escape but how the hell was I going to do that? I was one person. I faced at least one bent police officer and her assistant and an unknown amount of heavies. They were bound to have weapons too. I had nothing but my wits and my determination. Would it be enough to escape this place? In my favour I had the advantage of surprise though. They didn't know I was aware of the post mortem report and would not expect me to try and escape so would be off guard and relaxed. One thing was for sure though - the gloves were off now. I needn't play by any rules and I would do whatever it took to escape and commence my own investigation into what was going on. By sheer will alone I was determined to change the balance of power here. I would see to it, if I could, that proper justice is served and if anyone stood in my way, well they had better be prepared for a hard fight.

6

The great escape

My solicitor had left the room some time ago and now I was just waiting for the door to open and the Investigating Officers, Burton and her bag man, Link to take me to whatever interview room they had in this place. No doubt right now they were putting the final touches to their interview strategy which was bound to be underhand. This didn't worry me too much. I have always been too clever and on the ball for underhand PSD interview tactics and besides, they were making up their own evidence to prosecute me anyway. My thoughts were not so much on the interview but thinking about when I could make my move to attempt to escape. It was going to be very hard and I would probably not be able to escape but I had to try. I considered the possibility of escape in the interview but it would depend on the room, the layout, would they have any heavies in there with them? Etc. I just had to play it by ear and ride it on the seat of my pants. I knew nothing about the building I was in or the people in it. I just had to keep alert and on the look out for any opportunities that may or may not present themselves.

10 minutes had passed and I could hear a key in the door, bolts being slid back at the top and bottom of the door. The door opened. It was Link. He had a heavy with him. This was the first time Link had spoken to me.

"Follow me Lucas, Inspector Burton is waiting for you in the interview room."

I got off my bed and walked up to him. Link turned around and walked with his back to me. He was clearly either in his comfort zone or just sloppy as he did not assume I might attack but then Link had already proven sloppy by leaving his open brief case unattended earlier. This was not the moment to attack though, the heavy was behind me as I walked out into a lit corridor with what looked like metal walls interspersed by doors like the one I had come from every 12 feet or so. The corridor seemed to go on forever in both directions. There were also CCTV cameras dotted around. The heavy was carrying two weapons on a belt, one was a large wooden baton, the type police use to control rioters and the second weapon was what looked like a pistol. It looked like it was a Taser gun of some sort. What did interest me about that weapon though was that it wasn't secured to the heavy with a cord so if he dropped it, it would no longer be attached to him. The only thing securing the gun in place was what appeared to be a Velcro fastened strip.

We came to an open doorway on the left which was only a wooden door. There was a red light outside the door with a sign displaying, 'Interview room 3. When red light is on interview is in progress'.

"In you go" said Link gesturing with his hand.

I could see my solicitor sitting waiting behind a table for me looking more uncomfortable than I had ever seen him before. In front of him was Inspector Burton facing away from me at the opposing end of the table. On the table was a tape machine just like the ones used in police custody centres throughout the country.

"Come in PC Lucas, come in" said Burton without turning around.

I knew where I had to sit, the other side of Burton between my solicitor and the tape machine. I took my chair. Link sat down next to Burton and the heavy closed the door. There was a window in the door and I could see him take a position standing next to the door. He had not locked the door.

On commencement of the interview the tape machine was turned on, Burton covered all the legal aspects about why I was here, what I had been arrested for, she went over the caution again and my basic rights in custody. Once this had been done and my solicitor had introduced himself he said straight away, "My client knows that he is here on an extremely serious allegation that will have far reaching effects on his liberty. Bearing this in mind and also the fact that it has been some 4 weeks or so since the time of death of the apparent victim, may we see a copy of the Coroner's report please?"

Link cast a worried look at Burton as she replied, "This is not part of our disclosure to you."

My solicitor said, "Indeed it is your prerogative to choose to disclose what you wish as all in this room know but considering the severity of the allegation I would suggest that if you did not disclose this piece of evidence at this stage you could be damaging your own case in the eyes of the court. After all, why would you wish to hide this from us?"

Burton replied, "We do not have a copy of the post mortem or Coroner's report."

"So be it" said my solicitor.

Lots of questions were asked of me, many irrelevant like, "How long have you been a police officer?" and "How long has it been since your last personal safety training?" I did not answer the silly questions like that. I chose to answer and elaborate on questions I considered relevant so my side of events was put across without any PSD clouding around the edges. Inspector Burton was asking the questions leading the interview and Link was clarifying and going over what had been said at various points.

Link did himself no favours at all when at one point whilst clarifying what I had told him, he said, "… and you said that when he swung the knife the third time, that was when you said you had decided to kill him instead of being killed yourself..."

I immediately interrupted him and said, "No I didn't say that. What I said was that when it was becoming clear he was trying to kill me, I decided to punch him in the jaw to stop his attack on me."

This was a typical dirty interview tactic, what he was trying to do was get me used to answering, "yes, yes, yes, yes …" in the hope that I wouldn't notice what he had said and just said "yes" again on auto pilot and in so doing make an admission on tape to something I hadn't done. I really didn't like Link very much, or Burton either for that matter. They were acting the goodies but it was quite clear to me who the goodies and baddies were here.

Once the interview was concluded some unnecessary three hours later, Burton and Link left the room. My solicitor and I were left in the room with the heavy who was by now looking quite tired and bored. The heavy was a very big man, well over 6'5" tall; he was clearly a body builder with every muscle above his waist visible through the t-shirt that was far too tight. He had a neck like an ox and just looked to be made of pure solid muscle. His biceps were bigger than my head and he didn't look a friendly man either. This was the only opportunity I would get though and I knew that I was a skilled fighter, I had no idea of his skill level or if he even knew how to fight. I really hoped he was all show and no go but I knew this was unlikely. Sod it …

I covered the distance to the unsuspecting heavy in what is known in competition martial arts as the 'blitz' technique. It involves you running at the opponent with several hard and fast punches overwhelming them before they have even known what has happened. It is similar to what the Parachute Regiment call 'milling' but it is far more refined, precise and trained. I hit him with several punches starting in his solar plexus to try and wind him and then moving up to his nose to break it and ruin his vision. Every punch that hit his body felt like I was hitting a solid wall but I was knocking him backwards further with each blow, the punch on his nose broke it and blood spurted out every where. The heavy was knocked into a corner. He was still distracted with the surprise and ferocity of my attack. I reached down for his Taser gun at his belt. I couldn't get the bloody thing out. It wouldn't budge. This gave the heavy time to react. He roared out loud and threw me bodily backwards over the table. The table went over and me with it. I caught a glimpse of my solicitor - he was looking very shocked. I don't suppose he was expecting me to make an escape attempt at that moment. I looked back at the heavy and saw him draw the Taser gun. He was too slow. I covered the distance again and caught the hand holding the Taser gun with my left forearm pushing upwards. I then used my right hand to grab my left wrist to add leverage with my right arm behind his upper arm and forced his gun hand over his shoulder causing him pain and forcing him to drop the weapon. I then kicked the side of his right knee as hard as I could and heard a crack as he went down to the floor screaming. Next, I grabbed him around the neck and strangled him in a choke hold preventing him from breathing. I did this until he went unconscious and then I let go. I didn't want to kill him, just incapacitate him.

"Bloody good show Mr Lucas, but you could have waited until I was gone" said my solicitor. He was smiling now. "You took my advice, good."

"Yes," I said "but what the hell am I going to do now?"

It was at that moment that Link came into the room. He was clearly shocked to see the heavy unconscious on the floor. I grabbed him by his shirt and the back of his head and shoved him nose first into the wall as hard as I could. His nose burst open with blood. I then took him straight into a choke hold and did the same with him as I did to the heavy. He flopped down to the floor. Then Inspector Burton came in looking even more shocked to see her bag man and her heavy on the floor sparked out. I slammed the door shut.

"You wouldn't hit a woman would you?" she said as I saw her taking what looked like CS spray from a jacket pocket… bang, bang!! I knelt down and hit her straight in the solar plexus with a left cross winding her and then I came back up, swivelling on my toes and hit her in the jaw with a full power right hook, my most lethal punch. She went down instantly asleep.

"We don't tolerate sexism in the Police Force Burton," I said.

I put Burton on top of Link and the heavy and took her CS spray and the heavy's Taser gun.

What to do next? No alarm had been raised but I had to assume someone might have heard the commotion. I thought about taking the heavies clothing as a disguise but it wasn't a very good disguise and his trousers would be too long and his t-shirt, tight on him would be like a tent on me so that was a non-starter really. Anyway, at least I had the Taser gun and the CS spray. I had not been trained to use a Taser gun and this was the first time I had seen one in the flesh. It appeared to have a safety catch and a trigger so that was quite obvious. I knew that when activated, metal prongs would fire out and a very high voltage would discharge into the chosen target – not rocket science surely. I decided to also take the heavy's long wooden baton. I was now fairly tooled up for someone in custody. The odds were beginning to sway in my favour.

The other thing I needed to do if possible was find Link's brief case. To find that with the Coroner's report before I leave was something I had to try and do as that proved my innocence. I had to have that report.

"Mr Lucas, I will stay here on my chair. I can't be seen to assist your escape. Hopefully we will speak again soon. Good luck my friend," my solicitor said.

With that I nodded my goodbye to him and tentatively stepped out of the room.

What a fool that Link bloke was, very sloppy indeed, one could say he was the weak link in the chain; his brief case was right outside the door. I quickly opened it and found a document entitled: 'Mitchell Connor, DOB: 13/10/85 Post Mortem Report. Top secret.' Bingo! The document was too big to fold up and put in a pocket so I closed up the brief case and took the whole lot – there might be something else of use to me in there too. Now to get out; I walked down the corridor to its left, I didn't know which way was out so it was 50/50.

I had the Taser gun in my waist band of my jeans, the CS spray in a pocket. I carried the baton in my right hand and Link's brief case in my left. I was aware of the CCTV cameras, there was nothing I could do about them. I just had to hope that no one was paying them any attention right now. The corridor swept round to the right and as I rounded the corner I could see that about 60 yards further there was what looked like a wider, brighter lit room. I really hoped this was the right way. I walked as quietly as I could whilst trying to make my foot steps light and silent, but to my ears I sounded like an elephant stomping down the corridor. I could hear my heart beating loud and fast in my head like a bongo drum.

I got closer to the room and I could hear talking. I crept ever closer and peered round into the room. I could see three of the heavies in their black t-shirt uniforms. There was a desk behind them of some sort. They all looked relaxed and obviously had no clue as to what was going on. There was no way I could get past all that lot, they were all at least as big and muscular as the heavy I dropped in the interview room. I couldn't fight them all. I pulled the CS spray from my pocket. CS spray is an incapacitant. It will not cause any injury or marking unless you are within about one foot from the nozzle when it is discharged, the accelerant in the spray will burn the skin. The primary target is the eyes and face. It completely burns your eyes and nose without causing long term harm and will work on most people. It feels like someone has got the worlds hottest chilli peppers and rubbed them into your eyes but worse. It certainly works on me, I hate the stuff. Because of this I preferred not to use it at work if possible as it can affect you too if you spray it on someone. Spraying it in an enclosed space is very effective if you want to spray multiple targets but you obviously need to be prepared for it to affect you too.

I could see just past the heavies, day light the other side of a metal barred door. I assumed this door was locked and that at least one of those heavies must have the key.

I walked casually up to the heavies and said, "Hello." They all turned around. I held up the CS spray and emptied the whole can in their faces. They all dropped down to the floor, snot pouring out of their noses. That is all except one. "Fuck," I thought. Apparently there are a small proportion of people that are not affected by CS. This man was obviously one of them. I don't know why but he didn't seem to consider using his Taser gun or his baton, he just ran at me and punched me full on in my face. I couldn't avoid it, he was too fast. Next thing I could just feel my eyes and nose burning, the CS was affecting me too. I couldn't see and I dropped the brief case and baton. I could feel arms grab hold of me and squeeze me into a crushing bear hug. It took my breath away. I flung my head forwards and by complete luck made contact with something that felt soft. I heard a cry of pain and the arms holding me let go. I still couldn't see properly so I just rushed forward and guessed at where the man's head was. I found it in both my hands; I cradled his head in my hands and felt with my thumbs for his eye sockets. I then dug in my thumbs hard. I could feel his eyes being pushed inwards. He was screaming, "Stop, stop, please."

My hands felt something warm and wet running down them, blood. I was beginning to be able to see again. I kicked the heavy backwards with a hard front kick and pulled out my Taser gun. The heavy fell to the floor. I stopped just short of his legs and I aimed the gun at his groin.

I said, "Give me the keys to get out of here or I will fry your bollocks with this." I could see now he was bleeding from his eyes and nose. He pulled out a set of keys and slid them along the floor to me.

"This jobs not worth this shit for, take them, I'm sure they will catch up with you anyway."

"Thank you" I said, "now if you will also throw your weapons as far away from you as possible, I'm still pointing my Taser at your bollocks. Tell your colleagues to do likewise."

They had all heard me anyway and they obviously cared for their colleagues wedding tackle as they all did as I asked.

"Don't follow" I said, "I'm very determined."

I took the keys and picked the briefcase back up, all the while pointing the Taser gun at the heavy. Then I turned and sprinted to the barred door. I got to the door and turned around gun in hand. They were rushing now to the desk and I heard an alarm sound just as I put the key in the door and opened it. I ran outside. Day light! I was free from the building. All I could see was hills around me and tree's. I had no idea where I was. What would I do now?

7

At large

I looked behind me at the building I had just left. There was no building, what I was looking at was an opening cut into a hill with a barred door set five foot into it. Some 'special detention centre' that was, why had I been brought here? What a strange place.

There were just trees everywhere this side of the place. I ran to my right around the base of the hill entrance. I could now see a perimeter fence just behind some trees to my left with barbed wire over the top. The fence must have been about twenty feet high.

As I ran around the hill I could see now that there was a small car park. At the end of the car park there was a barrier with a security hut. There were only about eight cars in the car park but standing right in front of me were two security guards. They were wearing white shirts with epaulets and ties and looked out of shape and one of them in particular was a more elderly type. Not as threatening as the tooled up heavies in the building but there were two of them and I needed to get as far away from here as quickly as possible. There was no time to mess around being gentle with them. They were approaching me and the younger one of the two shouted, "Stop where you are."

I was still holding the Taser gun in my right hand and they were both walking up to me side by side with a look of intention on their faces. They were about 10 feet from me when I flicked the safety catch off on the Taser, lifted it up. I aimed it at the younger man straight into the centre of his body and pulled the trigger. There was a crack as the metal prongs shot out and connected with the security guard. He stopped dead in his tracks frozen as his body convulsed, he then dropped down.
I threw the weapon down as the other guard just stood open mouthed looking at his colleague. I lifted up my right knee, swivelled on my left foot, twisted my hips and stamped out a side kick straight into the older guards ribs. The kick was more than powerful enough to crack a rib or two. The kick took the guard straight off his feet and he landed on the ground on his backside. He was gasping for air and looked to be in pain. I didn't think the two of them were going to be getting back up very quickly.

I took a few steps away from the two disabled guards and opened Link's brief case. I thought I saw a set of keys in there when I opened it earlier... yes, there they were, a set of BMW keys. I had a look around the car park for anything that looked like a BMW. There was only one BMW in the car park, a new M3. The registration number looked like it spelt Link's surname but I didn't have time to work out how. I pressed the key fob and the doors unlocked. How on earth can a PSD caseworker like Link afford a new BMW M3? I guessed when he retired from the police he would have had some cash or maybe he invested in property?

I didn't dwell too much on Link's financial situation; I ran over to the security hut and found a green button which I pressed. This raised the barrier. I ran back to the M3, fired it up and drove out of the car park. I was free from the grounds of the 'special detention' centre and I was free for the time being. Technically I was at large; I would be a wanted man. PSD would be circulating me as wanted right now. This means that if I was stopped by police and they did a check on me on the Police National Computer (PNC) I would come back as 'wanted' and they would have to arrest me. A police officer would use whatever level of force necessary to affect my arrest as is their duty. I really didn't want to be in a position where I had to fight a police officer like me just going about his lawful duty – it might be ok for PSD to treat their colleagues badly but I'm better than them. I buried the accelerator pedal of the M3 right to the floor. I was driving flat out. I wanted to get as far as possible from this place as quickly as possible and I was in the right sort of vehicle to do that. I braked for the corners and judged the maximum speed as I entered, feathered the throttle round the corners to balance the car and squeezed it right to the floor again on the exits. The tyres of the car were just chirping away round the corners so I was as close as I dared to get to the cornering limits of an unfamiliar car. I drove like this on windy country lanes I did not recognise for about thirty minutes before I eased up on the accelerator although I still kept the pace quite fast. I took in my surroundings a bit more now I wasn't driving flat out, I was in an area surrounded by hills and greenery. I had to get rid of this car. The police would be looking for it and the number plates were a bit obvious. Also a car like this would probably have a Tracker device fitted. As I was deciding what to do with the car I was driving down a steep hill with a lake on the right hand side. I made my mind up. I would dispose of the car in the lake.

I stopped the car and had a look around. About 300 yards away I could see a little slope going into the lake for people to put their boats into the water. I drove slowly up to it, lined the car up with the slope and sped up; I then opened the door and jumped out with Link's brief case. I landed heavily on the floor and watched as the car crashed in to the lake sending a wave of water up ahead of it. The car kind of floated forward a few feet and then began slowly sinking, "That'll serve that bastard right" I thought as Link's new BMW M3 sank into the dirty water.

I glanced around; there were no people nearby to

witness my crime. I was still surrounded by hills. I really didn't know where I was at all as I had seen no road signs yet. I had never been a wanted man before and I hadn't really considered this as a possible situation so was still trying to think of what to do. Where to go? I couldn't go home as the PSD would be covering that. I couldn't go to any relatives or friends places, as again PSD would have that covered. I decided I needed to find somewhere where I could eat, rest, think and consider my options. I opened up Link's brief case again to see what else there was of use: A wallet with debit cards, credit cards and £300 cash. I chucked the cards into the lake – they would be no good as he would have cancelled those straight away and I could also be traced if I used them. The cash however was a life saver as I had £300 of untraceable spending power. The other item of use in the brief case was a mobile phone. Again I could be traced if I used this phone but I considered that if Links car had a Tracker device, they could know my current location anyway and I really wanted to speak to Louise to make sure she was ok.

I called Louise on the phone.

"Hello?" Louise answered her phone. She sounded very tired, quiet and quite subdued.

"Louise it's me, Jack"

"Jack! Oh my god, are you ok? I haven't heard from you

in so long," Louise's voice picked up in volume at the sound of my voice, she then broke down in tears.

I tried to hold back the tears unsuccessfully but I cried too, "I've been dying to speak to you Louise! Are you and Mollie ok? Is our baby ok?"

"I'm fine apart from worrying about you Jack. Baby is fine I think. We have told Mollie that you have had to go away with work so she is none the wiser" Louise said.

I replied, "Good, I'm glad things are ok. I'm ok at the moment but I'm on the run. They have made up evidence that I killed Connor and I have found out that his death was nothing to do with me. They're fitting me up Louise but I have the evidence that will clear my name in my hands right now, I just need to get it to the right people but they are after me!"

"Oh my God Jack, how can they do this to us?" said Louise.

"I don't know but I will clear my name. I can't talk long as they'll be listening. I will be back in contact again as soon as I can. I love you forever Louise whatever happens."

Louise replied, "Love you too Jack."

I then terminated the call and threw the phone into the lake.

I walked out to the side of the road and walked along with my thumb held out. I was going to try and hitch a lift.

8

The reluctant hiker

Saturday 8th September 2007 1900 hours

I had been walking along with my thumb held out for about only half an hour when a car stopped and the elderly couple inside invited me in, "Where are you going son? I can only take you as far as Lancaster as that's where we are headed." The road was going in a southerly direction, I could only guess I was somewhere in the Lake District. My geography of this area was not very good. "Lancaster is fine, thank you very much for stopping."

I was very lucky. I had been travelling in their car for only ten minutes or so when a police car shot by going the other way with its sirens and blue lights activated. I guessed that the crew in the car were on their way to a Tracker activation from Link's BMW and as far as they were concerned, thought they were looking for a petty car thief. I wonder what they would have thought if they knew they were looking for a fellow police officer running away from PSD.

The elderly man turned to his female companion and said, "Gosh they were in a hurry weren't they?"

The female then said, "My yes they were. I hope no one is in trouble."

"Well they will be when those boys catch them," said the male in return as he cackled a little laugh.

"Looked like they meant business," I added to their conversation.

"They certainly did," said the female "our grandson has just joined the police. We are very proud of him."

"He's been stationed at Leeds," added the male, "and is about to start work on the beat this week."

I thought back to my days when I just joined, I was a bit more worldly wise than most, but in relation to my expectations of the police I was naïve in the extreme, but then there is so much they don't tell you when you join up that they really should.

"Sorry," I said, "I should have introduced myself, my name's Jim. I'm a big supporter of our boys in blue too" I gave a big smile as the male turned around briefly,

"Pleasure to meet you Jim, I'm Gerald, this is my wife Mabel."

It took maybe half an hour to forty minutes to get to Lancaster. Gerald and Mabel seemed very nice. I told them I was on a hitchhiking holiday up north to get away from my stressful London job as a stockbroker. Gerald pointed out that it was unusual for a hitchhiker to have a brief case instead of a rucksack. I didn't elaborate on that as I couldn't think of any reasonable explanation for carrying a brief case instead of a rucksack. I asked Gerald if he knew of any cheap b&b's I might be able to stay in and he stopped outside a place called 'The Fishermans Rest'. I thanked him and offered him £30 of Nick Link's ill earned gains but he declined.

"Enjoy the rest of your holiday up north," Gerald said through his open window with a smile as he drove away.

The moment Gerald and Mabel were out of sight, I walked away from 'The Fishermans rest' in search of another place to stay. I did this just in case any questions may have been asked of them; in a situation where PSD traced them they would have told PSD who they would believe to be honest and decent police officers exactly where they dropped me off.

I found another b&b about 5 streets over and I booked myself in under the name Samuel Safe. I hoped I was safe. I went up to my room, flung the brief case down on the floor and collapsed on the bed exhausted... I fell asleep. I dreamt of Louise and our children.

9

Respite

Sunday 9ᵗʰ September 2007 0800 hours

I woke up with a start. I was having a nightmare … The judge saying, "Mr Lucas we find you guilty of Manslaughter" then court security taking me to a van and driving me to prison not to have any time with my family for a very long time. I looked around me at the b&b room and reality returned to me. My initial feeling was a deep upset that I couldn't just go home to Louise and Mollie then I felt a burning anger.

I was angry that Louise and Mollie were being put through this. We had a baby due very soon and we should be happy, excited and feeling secure not in this ridiculous situation. I felt angry that I had done the only thing I could when my life was on the line and used reasonable force in the circumstances and I was being made to face up to an allegation of Manslaughter. I shouldn't have been investigated for assault let alone Manslaughter. Even if Connor had died as a result of me defending myself against his manic knife attack on me then I am sure the law and the British public would support deadly force used in those circumstances – it was me or him. The fact that he didn't die as a result of my self defence was even worse. I always knew PSD could be malicious and liked to twist stories around to mess up the lives of the frontline police officers but I would never have imagined even in my wildest dreams that they would make up evidence to put a Manslaughter prosecution to a decent police officer knowing full well the death of the person was nothing to do with any dealings he had. I remembered Louise telling me I should have a medal for the incident. You are more likely to get a medal in the police though for making some stupid new politically correct rule that makes real policing more difficult or for recruiting the first blind female Mongolian lesbian officer into the firearms unit because they are under represented in that area - regardless of their suitability for the role. What a joke! I could handle giving my account in an interview and justifying my actions but things had gone a little too far here.

I checked myself; I had to focus on the task at hand. I had to somehow get the evidence I had to my solicitor but PSD knew I had the evidence. I had to suspect that all mail going to my solicitors' firm was being intercepted and opened. I really had to be very careful how I played things now. I considered that I would make a copy of the evidence and then hide the original copy of the report somewhere only I would know. I would then somehow get the copy to my solicitor. I couldn't stay here long and I had to be careful how I moved about. PSD would know that I was probably still in the vicinity and they would be monitoring public transport and key routes. I had to get a 'disguise' of some sort and new clothing. I made a list of things I needed with a pen and paper from Link's brief case. Then I took a shower.

I looked at myself in the mirror of the bathroom. I looked a bit of a state to be fair. I had a bruised and cut cheek bone where the heavy had thumped me. I had a bit of beard stubble and decided I was going to try and grow a beard. Any photographs of me that would be circulated to local police forces would show me clean shaven and a beard completely changes a face. My hair was already very short so there was no point cutting it.

After a shower I went out into Lancaster with Link's money. I bought a pair of sun glasses which I put on immediately on leaving the shop. It was a sunny day so they didn't look out of place at all. I then went to a camping shop and bought a rucksack, a water proof coat, three t-shirts, two pairs of combat trousers, a good pair of walking boots, a torch and several Kendal mint cakes. Next I went into a supermarket and bought lots of Yorkies, Mars Bars, Snickers bars, two big bottles of mineral water and a plastic lunch box container. I kept the plastic shopping bag also. I then found a library where I paid for the use of their photocopier and I made a copy of Connor's post mortem report.

I stuffed everything into my new rucksack and went back to my b&b. I changed into some of my new clothes. Everything else, I carefully packed away in the rucksack. I then went down to check out of the b&b and pay for my stay with Link's money.

I walked up to the reception desk. There was a local radio station blaring out the old song, 'When the going gets tough' by Billy Ocean. The owner who seemed a very talkative jolly old fellow was singing and dancing to it behind the desk. He looked up and saw me and stopped gyrating. He gave me an ever so slightly embarrassed look as he reached across to turn down the radio a bit.

"Sorry Mr Safe," he said, "I get a bit carried away when I hear that track. Did you sleep well? Is the room ok?"

He had a memory for names. I thought it was just as well I gave him a false name.

"I slept very well indeed thank you very much. The room was really nice, very comfortable. I would like to check out now please if that is ok?" I replied.

"Of course," the owner said.

He passed me the bill and I handed over the cash. I was just turning to leave when the owner said, "Oh Mr Safe, before you go there was something on the radio earlier it might be worth knowing. There was an urgent bulletin about some mad man that has escaped from a mental home in the area. Police say he is very dangerous and to stay well away from him if seen but to call police straight away. They gave a description of him but I didn't hear it as the phone went at that moment and I had to answer it. I just caught the end of his name. They said he was called Lucas. Bit of a worry, a mad man on the loose!"

My blood froze in my veins. I hoped he hadn't noticed any change in my appearance as I tried to recover as quickly as I could.

"I'll keep my eyes out for dangerous people. Thanks for the warning," I said as I smiled at him.

I walked out onto the street. I was worried. I knew now after the information that had just been relayed to me that police units in the area would be out proactively searching for me in the streets. As soon as they saw anyone matching my description they would stop check them. I had decided to try and make my way to the river. I knew there was a river somewhere in Lancaster and I had an idea that I may be able to take a boat of some sort and go along the coast, stop off somewhere like Cornwall and then make my way across land after somehow arranging a meeting with my solicitor where I could hand over the evidence for him to begin an offensive legal attack on PSD or at least, Burton and Link and of course in the process, completely exonerate me.

It was as I was trying to find the way to the river however that I walked past an old car for sale. It was an old grey Renault Clio, N reg, £200 ono 'enquire within or phone ....'" I had £150 left. It was the sort of car no one would look twice at and all I needed was something to get me a few hundred miles then I would abandon it. Perfect. I knocked on the door of the house and a frail old man who must have been in his nineties answered the door.

"Yes?" he said, he looked a bit irritable.

"I would like to buy your car out there but I haven't got £200. I have £150 though."

All of a sudden the old man sprang to life and seemed to perk up.

"One hundred and ninety pounds and you can drive her away right now," said the old boy.

I replied, "I'm ever so sorry but I really only have £150." I showed all the cash to the old boy, he took it from my hand and scrutinised it, holding one of the £20 notes up to the sky to check it was real, he was looking irritable again. I suspected he was tempted by the sight of the cash but really didn't want to let the car go for £150.

"You've got a cheek. That car there has served me fine since I brought her brand new for six thousand pound. She's a limited edition Oasis model you know…" his eye brow lifted at that moment as if I would be impressed "…and you want to take her away for one hundred and fifty."

"Yes," I replied.

"Ok," said the old man, "here's the key," and with that he shoved the car key in my hand and slammed the door shut. No log book or service history or anything, just the key and there you go, wham bam thank you ma'am. Oh well, not how I would normally do a deal on a car but it wasn't my money anyway. If it didn't start though, then I would be knocking on his door again for my money back. The car started, however, on the button and appeared to be relatively well kept. I pulled away, the proud new owner of a grey N registration Renault Clio Oasis diesel. It even had a full tank of fuel thrown in with the deal.

10

The road to hell

Sunday 9th September 2007 0800 hours

I drove towards the M6 as I knew this would take me as far south as the Midlands and then further south via the M40 / M42. A risky route as I imagined the Road Policing Units of the motorway network would have been made very aware of me as a wanted man that would likely be using this route southbound. I hoped however, that my grey Renault Clio would go largely unnoticed at a good steady 75 mph. It was a sunny day again so I could wear my sunglasses and not look out of place.

I switched on the radio. I wanted to hear the local stations to see if I could hear what was being said about me. I swapped radio stations for about fifteen minutes before I found what I was searching for. I was listening to a station called 'The Northern Lights' when it was broadcast ...

A male newsreaders voice announced, "We apologise

for the interruption in broadcast to bring an urgent bulletin. An extremely dangerous man named Jack Lucas has escaped from a secure ward of the Lancaster Department of Psychiatry. The public are warned not to approach this man as he is extremely unstable. Police believe that he is capable of extreme and unprovoked violence and warn that if seen police should be contacted immediately on 999. This man is described as white in colour, aged in his mid thirties with short brown hair. He is of a medium build and approximately five foot eight inches tall. The public are warned that he is extremely volatile and he should not be approached. A photograph of him is available to view on our website and also on …"

I had heard enough, I switched the radio off.

So I had gone from a police officer to a criminal and now to a nutter who was a danger to all society.

There isn't much to say about driving down the M6 in an old diesel Renault Clio. It is a very dull route but it gave me lots of time to think. I was so worried about Louise and that all of this could make serious complications in her pregnancy. I wanted to call her but I had no phone and her phone number would, without doubt be being monitored by PSD. I thought that at some stage I might be able to buy a pay as you go type phone from a supermarket and a few SIM cards so I would always be calling on a different number when I phoned her but I had no money now. I gave my last £150 for the car. I ate one of my Mars Bars and sipped from a bottle of mineral water as I drove. I realised that I had to stash the original copy of Connor's post mortem report ASAP. I didn't want to get caught with it. That report was my lifeline, the only thing that would get me out of this mess and turn the tables on the PSD Officers Burton and Link.

I had been travelling for some time and I could see sign posts telling me Keele Services was approaching. I was about to take a very measured risk. There could easily be a police patrol car in the service station checking lorries or stopping for their KFC but I was going to stop anyway. I had to stop somewhere soon to do this so I decided to do it now. It wasn't a call of nature I was stopping for but I was planning on killing two birds with one stone and emptying my bladder at the same time.

I pulled into the main car park of the service station, found a space between two cars, reversed into it and stopped. I switched the engine off and then leant into the front passenger seat for my rucksack. From that I pulled out the plastic lunch box, the supermarket bag and the original copy of Connor's post mortem report. I folded the evidence in half so it fit into the lunch box, sealed the air tight top and then put it in the supermarket bag. I then tied the ends of the bag tight. Then I stepped out of the car and looked around, there were few people about and they were closer to the service station entrance, they wouldn't notice me. I walked to the edge of the car park towards some trees that were set back in a flower bed with lots of thick bushes. I counted the lamp posts along the edge of the car park. I was near the third lamp post to the left of the corner of the car park. I checked again that no one could see me and I walked into the bushes and trees. I walked approximately eight paces into the foliage. I was hidden from any public view now. I was near a tree and could not walk any further as there was a steep bank going upwards from this position. I quickly attended my call of nature and then I bent down at the base of the tree and dug a hole in the ground using my hands. I dug approximately one foot down and then I placed the supermarket bag containing the lunch box into the hole and in that, the evidence that would hopefully be my life saver. I put all the soil back over and carefully patted the ground to make it look smooth. I put some stones over the top and pulled some nearby weeds over. Next I carved into the tree, a single straight line with my car key. I was ready to go back to the car.

I stepped out of the shrubbery and I was dismayed to see my new car had somehow drawn the attention of two HATO Officers. HATO stands for Highways Agency Traffic Officers. They are not police and they have no power in the field of crime and that includes traffic law. They do not have authority to access PNC (the Police National Computer) and they are not privy to information on criminals, wanted or otherwise. Nevertheless I was concerned as I did not want to draw the attention of anyone, especially not a government agency. They were looking at the windscreen of my car. I approached and said as politely as possible with a smile, "Hello gents, anything I can help you with?"

Both of the HATO Officers were aged in their 50's, one was short and fat, the other was tall and skinny. They looked a bit like Laurel and Hardy. The short fat one who looked like Hardy said "Is this your car?"

I replied, "Yes it is. I literally just bought it today why?"

Hardy then said in a really quite aggressive and unnecessary manner, "Well your tax disc is one month out of date! Do you know you are committing a road traffic offence?"

I was a bit taken aback. Even as a police officer that has a duty to deal with crime and traffic matters both serious and very minor I would never talk to someone in such an unprofessional and aggressive way, especially about something as minor as an out of date tax disc.

I replied to him, "You don't look much like a police officer to me."

He immediately retorted, "I am a Traffic Officer and you are committing a traffic offence."

I again replied, "The Highways Agency Traffic Officers are not authorised to deal with crime. I only bought the car today anyway. When I get home I will make sure the tax is sorted. You have no power to deal with this, now would you please leave me alone and step back from my car."

"We don't but the police do have a power, and we are going to report you. I require you to stay here with me while I call up for a police unit to deal with you," said Hardy.

"Look don't be silly," I said, "don't you think police have better things to deal with than this? It really doesn't require a police unit to attend, and on top of that, you have no power to keep me here." There wasn't much he could say to that as he really didn't have the power to keep me there.

I got in my car, switched on the engine and drove out of the space, as I manoeuvred the car, Hardy came running up to my driver's window shouting, "I have reported you! I have reported you! On my radio!"

I just drove off from the monkey but was now feeling extremely unnerved. It might only be a very trivial matter but he would have given out my registration number to his control room who in turn would be passing the information to the local police control room who would be obliged to send a unit to check me and my car if they came across me. A police unit would come across a lot more than a dodgy tax disc in doing so.

I continued my journey south towards Wessex; I had got as far as the A34 junction on the M40 incident free when disaster struck... Smoke started coming into the cars cabin through the air vents, there was a strong smell of something burning.

"Shit!" I exclaimed.

The level of smoke coming into the cabin was increasing and filling up the car. I saw a small flame lick out from under the bonnet. So much for not drawing attention to myself. I pulled over onto the hard shoulder, pulled out my rucksack and jumped out of the car coughing and spluttering, my lungs were full of the smell of burning. I ran away from the car a few feet and I was sick on the floor. I looked around at the car; the flames were spewing out of the engine bay now. A pillar of black smoke was billowing up into the air. People would be able to see this for miles around – I would now be the cause of a tail back and rubbernecking both sides of the M40 and there I was trying to go unnoticed. It was then I saw the BMW police patrol car pull up with blue lights activated.

11

The cavalry arrives

The police patrol car stopped about 100 metres from the back of my burning car. I had nowhere to run and if I did run I would be making myself a target for the officers in the car – they would assume I was a disqualified driver / drink driver / wanted criminal trying to get away and they would do their best to catch me. I had to stay here and try and blag my way through with false details.

Two officers got out of the car and ran towards me. They were running over to assess the situation and make sure that the occupant(s) of the car were ok. They would already have called up for the Fire Service to attend and now needed to establish if they would need an ambulance. I moved towards them a safe distance to the nearside of the burning car and waved as I moved further away from the car and closer to them. I had to appear as normal as possible; I didn't want to give them any reason to suspect there was anything unusual here.

"You all right?" said one of the officers.

"Yes thanks," I replied, "there is no one else in the car, just me and I'm ok."

"We have got Fire Service en route to deal with it. What happened?" asked the shorter of the two officers. They were both approximately in their mid 30's like me. One had a shaved head and the other was of Indian origin with spiky hair and a short beard, he was shorter than his shaven headed colleague. I could tell straight away these were good officers, the sort of blokes I liked to work with.

"The car just caught fire for no apparent reason at all. I only bought it this morning in Lancaster," I explained. I wanted to be honest about where I bought it as I knew a PNC check would probably show the cars registered owner as living in Lancaster.

"You ought to get your money back mate," said the larger shaven headed officer.

I laughed and they laughed with me.

The shorter officer then said, "Look we have a procedure we need to follow whilst we wait for the fire brigade to come and put the fire out. Have you got any ID on you at all?" He wanted to check my car and me on the PNC which is exactly what I would do in this situation.

"Sorry, all my ID is burning in the car," I replied.

"That's ok," said the shorter officer. "What is your name, please?"

"Samuel Safe," I replied.

"Thank you, and what is your date of birth please Mr Safe?"

I made up a date of birth, but kept the year of birth the same as mine. Whilst he was doing this the shaven headed officer wrote down the registration number of my car which was by now a burning inferno but the rear plate was still visible. He then gave his note book to his colleague who ran off a PNC check on his radio... I listened ...

"Romeo Tango zero one for a vehicle and person check please."

"Control to Romeo Tango zero one go ahead...." The shorter Officer read out the registration number of my car first and waited. Shortly a response came back from his control room,

"The vehicle comes back to an RO (Registered Owner) from Lancaster, a Mr Theodore Underhill of Alexandra Road. There is a report on the car, are you free to speak?"

Shit, this meant that there was some sort of marker on my vehicle. Hopefully it was just that idiot HATO and his issue with my out of date tax. The shorter officer then looked at me and turned his back on me as he walked two steps away. As he did this, the shaven headed officer stepped closer to me and turned his radio down. They did this just in case I was arrestable for some reason. They didn't want me to hear the radio and the shaven headed officer stepped closer in order to be able to grab me if he needed. I saw the shorter officer shaking his head. He turned around and came back up to me with a smile on his face.

"Apparently you had a run in with one of our lovely HATO Officers and you have no tax."

"Yes," I replied.

"Like you said, though, you only just bought the car and now it's gone up in flames. I think I'll let you off that heinous crime although the HATO would probably like to see you hang for that."

Again we all laughed, these two were good blokes. "I checked you out on the radio as well and you are not known to us so you'll be pleased to hear we won't have to arrest you."

He said this in a jokey manner and I could tell he was

only trying to calm my nerves after the car fire. Their radios came to life again.

"Control to Romeo Tango zero one are you still with your stop check?"

The shorter Officer responded, "Answer: yes."

The control room came back on "Control to Romeo Tango zero one, you have been requested by the force control room Inspector to keep your subject where he is. Another unit needs to talk to the male. Can you confirm a description of him?"

The shorter Officer gave a description of me on the radio to his control room and then added "… what unit is it that wants to talk to him? Will they be in a marked vehicle?"

The control room responded, "Unknown, wait one and I will get back to you." Bastards! That unit was bound to be PSD; they have somehow linked the name Samuel Safe or the vehicle to me.

I didn't have many options here. These two officers were good lads. I didn't want to give them the same treatment as the PSD cronies from the strange detention centre, but at the same time if I told them the truth they would still have a job to do.

Suddenly there was a screech of tyres on tarmac and

then an almighty bang and the sound of broken glass and crunching metal. All three of us turned to look in the direction of the noise. One car had driven into another that had slowed down to look at my burning wreck of a car. It was a pretty big collision and the car that had been struck rolled across the road onto its roof. This was my opportunity. The two officers would have no choice but to deal with the accident. It was a serious accident and they needed to deal with this ASAP.

I turned and ran off the motorway and into a field running alongside it.

12

Fields of Liberty

I sprinted as hard and fast as I could. I was running across the field and was getting closer now to the nearest hedge. I dived over and headed in the direction of a farm house. I ran parallel to another hedge as from the motorway someone would still be able to look into the fields, close to the hedge I would be more difficult to spot than if I was running through the middle of the field.

I got to the farm house and I ran past it and down hill. Now I was out of line of sight of the motorway. I kept running but slowed from a sprint now to a jog and found a pace I would be comfortable with long distance. I came to a railway line and ran across to the other side, more fields and then another farm house. I gave this house a wide berth as I didn't want any potential witnesses to a man fitting my description.

I could hear the sound of a helicopter. PSD had got the local force's air unit authorised to help them. I felt a surge of adrenaline; it is very tricky to escape the eye in the sky. "Just keep running," I thought to myself.

I carried on running over field, after field, after field. The place was littered with fields.

Through one field I could see a tractor working just the other side of a hedge. I really hoped the driver hadn't seen me but if he had there was nothing I could do about it now.

The light was starting to fade and so was I. I must have been running now for a good couple of hours across fields and I was so tired. I had been driving the country's dullest roads for hours and I had been running for a long time. I needed to find somewhere to rest. I found a small copse of trees alongside a field and carefully picked a spot that had cover overhead and around the sides. I took off my rucksack and collapsed to the floor. I drank from one of my water bottles and just sat still and listened. I could hear the sound of the helicopter in the distance; I guessed it must be a Thames Valley unit around here. The sound of the helicopter faded away in the distance. I then closed my eyes and fell asleep.

13

Sniffed out

I was dreaming of Louise. She was kissing me. Then she started licking my face like a dog. She licked my eye and was making a loud sniffing sound, what on earth? Louise changed into a dog, a German shepherd … I wasn't dreaming. It was a German shepherd!

I flinched back and the dog started barking and snarling manically at me but was pulled back by its keeper, a police dog handler. I focused and could see another male with the dog handler. Inspector Mann. Shit. He was dressed in civilian clothes. "Jack your luck has run out. I am further arresting you for Assault on Police times eight (the security guards and heavies would count as police for this offence as they were acting under police authorisation), Theft of Motor Vehicle, and Driving without insurance and Failure to display a valid tax disc."

Mann adding the tax disc offence on the end just shows

what sort of an arse hole this bloke is. He cautioned me and gave me the necessity of my arrest and then said, "this will go nicely with the Manslaughter charge won't it Jack. You're going down for a long time."

I replied, "You mean the made up charge of Manslaughter do you Mann?"

He didn't reply. Instead he opened up my rucksack and began searching it. He pulled out my copy of Connor's post mortem report and looked at me. He then said to the dog handler, "Would you leave us a minute? I need to speak to PC Lucas alone."

"Yes sir," replied the dog man.

Once the dog man was sufficiently far enough away, Mann opened up the documents and read it.

"A copy," he said, "where is the original, Jack?"

I just smiled at him and said, "You're in on it too eh along with Burton and Link? What are you lot trying to hide? Why am I being used as a scapegoat here? Am I being used to cover up someone else's incompetence?" I watched Mann's face. He looked angry and a little worried. I had hit a nerve.

"You're a little shit Jack, I have never liked you," said Mann with real venom in his voice,

"That's all right sir, the feeling's mutual," I replied. I then added, "Whatever happens to me, I would say that you and your cronies are in much deeper shit. You have no idea what I have done with the original copy of Connor's post mortem."

"You'll tell us," said Mann as he gave me a very evil looking smile.

The local police units' helicopter landed nearby and an officer stepped out of the aircraft. He was holding a Taser gun and it was pointing at me.

"You already know how these work I understand Jack," said Mann "You're coming with me in the helicopter but before you do, I'm going to put these on you."

Mann took out a pair of rigid handcuffs. He roughly turned me around to apply the handcuffs to me. I felt a surge of anger and I very nearly retaliated with force but the Taser totting officer was still pointing his weapon at me. I didn't fancy all that voltage so I allowed him to handcuff me. Once I was secured in handcuffs, Mann roughly pushed me in the direction of the waiting helicopter.

Then Mann did something extremely unprofessional. He kicked me on the back of my knee knocking me down. I landed on the floor unable to break my fall properly in the handcuffs. I turned my head to see

Mann rushing up to me. I then saw his foot draw back as if he was about to execute a football penalty kick. I saw a brief flash image of his foot an inch from my head, I felt the impact of his foot with my head and then everything went black briefly.

I felt confused. I forgot where I was and what was happening. I looked around and then I saw Mann again with a face contorted with anger, his eyes brows were close together, his face was red and he looked insane. I then quickly remembered what was going on as I saw him pulling his foot back to kick me again …

"Sir!" I heard the Taser totting officer shout. I looked across and could see the other officer was looking at Mann with a look of real concern. Mann looked across at him and said, "You never saw that. If you did your career will be over."

The officer looked at me and shook his head in disbelief. I could taste blood in my mouth and could feel a big lump forming on the side of my head where Mann kicked me. Mann then picked me up and walked me to the helicopter. The Taser officer stepped in with us, holstered his weapon and then just sat there in silence looking away from me and Mann.

The helicopter lifted into the air and then flew off in a southerly direction.

14

Old friends

We had only been in the air for a short time before the helicopter approached what looked like an RAF base. There were Chinook helicopters and a Hawk trainer jet parked up on the ground. The helicopter descended and as I looked out of the window I could see that there was a police van parked by the landing pad. That must be my taxi from here then.

The helicopter landed and Mann motioned for me to step out after the other officer. There were three police officers waiting outside the van.

As the three of us approached the police officers with the van one of them stepped up, he had Sergeant stripes on his epaulets.

"Hello sir," he said to Mann, "to Reading custody yes?"

Mann replied, "Yes for now Sergeant, he'll only be with you there for a short time before we take him away."

Take me away where? Hopefully not one of those strange special detention centres.

"What's going on, Mann? Where am I going after Reading?" I asked. Mann just ignored me and walked away towards a building.

I was put into the back of the van after I had been searched by one of the police officers. They tried to make small talk with me but I really wasn't in the mood to respond.

I was taken into Reading Police Station after a short drive and booked in just like any other criminal. I noted that the Detention Officers here were really good; they took my fingerprints on behalf of the officers. In Southmouth the lazy sods expect you to do everything. Wasn't helping me though, I was the prisoner, not the investigating officer.

I was booked into a cell and given a cup of tea by the DO.

Here I waited, again pondering on all my thoughts. My thoughts again returned to Louise and my family and I worried about them. I tried to think of how next to play the situation. What to do? I thought I might be able to phone my solicitor and tell him where the evidence was but PSD would be there before him and it would be gone. I couldn't do that. I had to see where they were taking me next and hope for another escape opportunity.

After about an hour and a half I guessed, the door was unlocked and opened. It was Inspector Burton and Nick Link. It amused me to see that Link's nose had a plaster on it and Burton had a seriously bruised and swollen jaw.

They had come to take me away to my next destination. Link said, "Out." Nothing else.

"What happened to your nose?" I said with a smile. I couldn't resist it.

Link ignored me.

I was booked out of Reading custody. Burton and Link took me outside to another van. This one was unmarked but it had a cage inside the back for prisoners and it was into this that I was placed.

The van was being driven fairly fast for approximately an hour and a half. I couldn't see where we were going. There were no windows in my cage. The only light was from a small electric light on the roof of the cage.

Eventually the van stopped and it sounded like we were at some sort of gate as I could just about hear Link's voice talking to someone outside the vehicle as something metallic sounding was dragged across the ground in front of the van. After a brief verbal exchange, the van moved off again slowly and then came to a stand still. I could hear several footsteps outside the back of the van, and then the doors were opened. The sight in front of me scared me... I was looking at about a dozen of the heavies in their black t-shirt uniforms. Immediately in front of them were Burton and Link. Behind all of them was a large disused looking warehouse.

Link turned to me, "Lucas, this is where you are going to talk. You are going to tell us where that report is you took. But before you talk, you are going to pay."

Two heavies grabbed me by my arms. I couldn't move even if I wanted to. Link then pulled a truncheon from his jacket. It was the old fashioned style truncheon that police stopped using years ago in the days of Dixon of Dock Green. Link then belted me in the ribs with it. It was excruciatingly painful and felt like it had cracked a rib or at least badly bruised my ribs. I would have doubled over with the pain but the heavies were holding me up and I couldn't. Link then said "That's for trashing my car Lucas, I am going to enjoy this."

I was then dragged into the warehouse by the two heavies.

15

The red carpet treatment

They hadn't exactly rolled out the red carpet for me, but it would be true to say that I was, at this precise moment in time, dangling over carpet which was red, red with my blood.

I was hanging by my arms which in turn were manacled to rusty chains dangling from the roof of the warehouse. It felt like my shoulders were going to pop out of my body. I had spent the last ten minutes being used as a live punch bag by one of the heavies. Apparently he was one of the ones I sprayed with CS at the detention centre. He only stopped hitting me because he hurt his hand on my head. It looked as if he had broken a knuckle. I bloody hoped so. I had taken quite a beating from him and the blood on the floor was from my nose and I think also from a reopened cut on my face. No questions had been asked of me yet.

All of a sudden I fell down and the chains holding me

up all fell on me in a rusty heap on the soiled carpet. I heard a voice behind me.

"Get up Jack."

I recognised the voice. I turned around. Mann, Burton and Link all stood together with two heavies behind them. It was Mann's voice. He continued, "So are you going to tell us now what you have done with the report we need?"

I replied, "Of course I'm not. It proves my innocence and your guilt. I would rather die than give you that and no amount of pain you put me in will make me tell you."

Mann did not reply to me. Instead he turned to the two heavies and said, "Dave, Frank go ahead."

The two heavies, Dave and Frank as I now knew them to be called, rushed over to me and hoisted me up bodily holding an arm each. They turned me around with the chains still attached to my wrists and ran with me in their hands over to what looked like a small pool of water in a horse's trough. All the while, the chains were dragging behind me on the floor. Dave and Frank didn't pause or stop; I just went face first into the water. They pushed me in deep, as far as my shoulders. I had time to get a deep breath of air before I went in as I could see what was coming. Subtle these guys were not.

They held me under for what seemed an age. I was really struggling to keep my breath held, my lungs were burning up but still they held me under. I had to breathe out but I kept trying to hold it. I couldn't hold it anymore, my body was forcing me to breathe out but still, I was being held under the water. I breathed out and just as I felt I had to take a breath in I was hauled out of the water.

All three of the bent PSD cronies were near me now and they were all smiling except Burton, I suspected her jaw was hurting too much to smile.

They gave me time to get my breath back and then Link said, "Tell us Lucas or they will put you in again."

I realised that I wouldn't take much of that treatment without drowning but there was no way I was going to tell these goons where the evidence was. "Fuck off you fat bastard!" I spat out.

Mann made a motion with his hand to Dave and Frank to the pool of water and in I went again…

This time they held me in for longer, I breathed in and got a lungful of water. They hauled me out and I was coughing up water and being violently sick. They took off my manacles and walked me over to an upright metal pole sticking up from the ground. I was handcuffed to this so that the pole was between me and the cuffs. I was facing outwards and was cuffed to the rear. Mann walked up to me and then cut my t-shirt open at the front using a knife which he then gave to Link.

Mann and Link then walked around behind me out of sight.

Everyone was behind me and they were being very quiet. I didn't know what was coming next. I heard the sound of something behind me like a gas burner catching light. I could also feel warmth as if someone had lit a large fire behind me. Mann then walked into my view. He was holding a long metal pole but it was what was connected to the end of it that I was worried about. At the end of the pole was a square metal slab, approximately 5 inches by 5 inches. It was glowing red hot and he was going to press it against the now bare skin of my torso. He held it close to my chest, within an inch. Even held away from my chest but so close, it felt like it was burning my skin as if it was pressed against me, I could feel and smell the hairs on my chest burning.

Mann then said, "Tell me where it is Jack and I won't do this."

I didn't reply.

He held back for about 5 seconds and then, satisfied I

wasn't going to tell him, he smiled that evil smile he gave me earlier when he caught me in the field. He then leant forward and pressed the hot metal slab firmly on my bare chest. The pain was excruciating, I howled out in pain as the metal slab sizzled on my chest. I could smell my skin burning like a piece of meat over cooking in an oven.

After a few seconds Mann removed the piece of metal. My skin felt like it was burning all over my upper chest. I was in absolute agony. I collapsed to the floor still attached to the metal pole with my hands cuffed behind me.

"That's it for today Jack. This is just a taster. When the sun comes up tomorrow if you do not tell us what we want to know you are going to get far worse than this. Think about it while we are asleep and hopefully by the time we see you in the morning, you will have made the right decision," said Mann.

Then they all left the warehouse leaving me attached to the pole by my hand cuffs.

I looked down at my chest, it was red raw. Where the metal slab had been pressed against my skin, there was a perfect square at a slight angle on my chest where it looked like it had burned all the way through to my pectoral muscle. It was still burning like mad. It felt awful. I looked up at the pole that I was cuffed to. I considered climbing it but I was facing the wrong way and I needed my hands which were hand cuffed behind me in the worst position. Even if I could miraculously climb up with just my legs, I would be walking around with my hands behind my back. There was no point trying. I just sat there hoping the pain in my chest would go away; I tried to rest and recuperate my energy. It got dark and I could hear an owl hooting not very far away. I didn't sleep much at all. I thought again of my family and felt dread in my stomach for what would come the next day.

16

Once bitten twice shy

Tuesday 11th September 2007 0800 hours

"Wakey, wakey!" came a loud shout. It was Mann's voice I opened my eyes and looked up. I saw Mann walk in with Link and the two heavies, Dave and Frank. Link was carrying a large wooden box. No doubt it had the day's torture instruments inside it. I wondered with morbid fascination what they would do to me today.

Mann spoke up again, "You have had your night to sit and think about whether you want to tell us where our report is. Well? Are you ready to tell us or would you prefer some more of our hospitality?"

I didn't answer. I wasn't going to tell them and at the same time I didn't want to wind them up any more than necessary. If today was going to be worse then yesterday then I really was in very deep shit indeed.

"Still not going to tell us then?" Link said

Then Mann continued, "Maybe this will change your mind."

Mann took the wooden box from Link and brought it over to me. He opened the top of the box and took out a glass case. The case had a small door on its side with what looked like a vice type clamp around it. I looked inside the case; I could see a spider web with a small black spider in the middle with an egg sack. There were red markings on the spider.

"Do you know what this is Jack? It's a female Black Widow spider, one of the most poisonous spiders in the world. She is guarding her eggs and is very protective. This bit here," he pointed to the small door on the side of the glass box "is where your hand is going to go. She will bite you and it will hurt, she has fangs like a snake you know, then the poison will go into you. You probably won't die as that is quite rare but you might do. After about twenty minutes you will have stomach cramps and muscle spasms. It is going to be excruciatingly painful. All you have to do to stop this is tell us where that report is Jack."

I remained silent. I am scared shitless of spiders. I don't mind the little house spiders or garden spiders we get in this country but I have always had a fear of poisonous spiders or big spiders. So much for the Human Rights Act!

Again, Mann waited for a few seconds for an answer as he studied me. I gave him none.

"Right then, Dave, Frank, Nick let's get started," Mann said.

Dave and Frank went behind me and took off the handcuffs. One of them, I wasn't sure which was Dave and which was Frank then put my left arm into an entangled arm lock which basically involves him folding his arm around my forearm whilst holding onto my upper arm with his hand. It can be an effective restraint technique. In this hold I was walked further down the warehouse to where I could see a chair and table waiting. Mann and Link ran in front and placed the spider case onto the table with the side door of it facing the chair. I was sat down forcibly on this chair by Dave and Frank. One of them stood behind me and held both of my hands flat on the table. He was so strong there was no way I could move. Whilst one of the goons did this, the other put on some thick rubber gloves and loosened up the vice clamp by the door of the box. Once this was done, Dave or Frank (I'm not sure which) carefully opened the side door of the box. As this was done, the spider suddenly moved, feeling its web with its front legs. Then Link and Mann together grabbed my right forearm, and assisted with one of the goons, they plunged my hand into the box. The clamp was then quickly tightened around my wrist so I couldn't remove my hand from the box. My hand was right in the spider's web. I tried to move my hand from the spider by swivelling it to the left in the box. Mann and Link had let go by this stage and it was only the heavy holding both my arms down still. All of a sudden the spider moved like lighting up to my hand, I saw it settle on one of my fingers, I tried to shake it off but I couldn't. Then I felt a searing pain in my index finger, the pain shot right up my arm. I screamed louder than I have ever done in my life. I looked at my hand and I could actually see the spider's fangs embedded in my finger. The physical pain was awful but the added psychological dimension of knowing that right now, at this precise moment in time, I was being bitten by a black widow spider was unbearable. I felt the arm holding down my right arm relax slightly.

"Fuck you!" I shouted and moved my arm slightly to the left.

The heavies grip on me now was gone. I swung the glass box still attached to me via the clamp up and over my head… There was a loud smash and the sound of glass landing on the floor. I was trying to smash it on the head of the man behind me. It worked. I spun around and simultaneously used my left hand in an open palm strike, and using the momentum of my spin for extra power; I struck the heavy in his chest. This sent him sprawling to the floor. I could see he was bleeding from his head and the spider was on his eye. He was screaming. He was obviously as scared of poisonous spiders as me.

He was preoccupied now but as I turned around, the

other heavy was moving into action. I could see Link and Mann backing off slightly. The heavy put his hands up in a boxing stance.

"Come on then Frank let's be having you," I said.

"It's Dave," he replied in a deep voice which sounded like the brain behind it was seriously lacking in IQ.

I then heard what must have been Frank's voice behind me.

"It bit me, the fucking thing bit me, help!"

Frank had an unusually high pitched voice that seemed at odds with his appearance – maybe the spider had bitten him on the bollocks.

Dave shuffled towards me and threw a clumsy left jab at my face. This was easy to avoid. I ducked down, and moved my head under and around the punch. I came back up and hit him square on his jaw with a right hook. This punch totally stunned Frank and I then followed this up with a left cross to his chin. I didn't want to mess around anymore. As far I was concerned it was 'anything goes'. I then jabbed him in his eyes with the tips of my left finger and punched him as hard as I could with a right cross straight into his Adams Apple. He went straight down making a gurgling noise and clutching at his throat and eyes. I then ran up to him fast and kicked him in his groin with the ends of my toes. My boots had steel toe caps.

I didn't think he would be getting up again in a hurry.

Frank and Dave down, now what about Link and Mann? I looked around; I could see the two of them running out of a warehouse door. I followed. I was determined to do some damage to at least one of them before getting away from here.

As I turned the corner by the door I could see them both running away between cargo containers of some sort. Link, being more fat and out of shape than Mann was lagging behind and running much slower than me. I quickened my pace and caught up with Link. I grabbed him by his jacket and pulled him around into a cargo crate. He started swinging wild punches at me in what could only be described as 'windmilling' whilst he closed his eyes in the vain hope that one might hit me. I just leant back and they all missed. I punched him in his solar plexus, winding him. He bent over and then pulled a long sharp knife from out of his jacket. It looked like a World War 2 Commando type dagger – it must be the knife Mann had used to cut open my t-shirt. Before he had a chance to do anything with it, I kicked it out of his hand with a turning kick using the instep of my right foot. The knife bounced off the crate to my left. Continuing the momentum from the right turning kick, I spun around and kicked Link again with my left foot using a spinning side kick. I stamped it straight under his chin into his neck. This took him off his feet and he landed on his bottom with a thump. He got up again and just ran at me. I waited for him to get within range of my hands and then I took his head in my hands. I grabbed his chin with my left hand and the top of his head with my right hand. I then pulled him towards me as I rotated his head by pushing up with my left hand and pulling down and clock ways with my right hand. Once I had Link in an unnatural position and his chin was pointing slightly upwards from his shoulders, I thrust my right hand forwards and pulled my left hand down. I could feel a big jolt in his neck accompanied with a loud knocking noise. I could feel that his spine was broken in his neck, his body went limp and I let it drop to the floor. Link was dead.

I gave Link's corpse a quick cursory search and found a mobile phone which I took.

I had never killed anyone before in my life. I didn't know how I would feel about killing Link in days to come, but right now I was just hoping his soul was burning in hell and felt no remorse whatsoever for his loss of life.

I moved away from the body. There was a tiny gap in the cargo crates to the right. It was barely big enough for me to get through. I sucked in my tummy and pulled my chest as flat as possible and I went through; I didn't want to go the same route as Mann took as by now I imagine I would be running into a wall of heavies.

Behind the crates was a fence immediately in front of me. It was only a few feet high and behind it was another yard with disused warehouses and scrap cars. I climbed over. I guessed the PSD cronies and their hired henchmen hadn't considered I might escape this way. I ran through the yard to the nearest warehouse and turned right. I wanted to put as many corners and objects between me and any pursuers as possible. I ran between two warehouses and then turned left along the front of another two. Here there was another small fence and a wooded area behind. I climbed over and dropped down the other side of the fence into the woods.

17

The devil's chariot

I moved through the woods as fast as I could. It was very overgrown and I was getting cut left, right and centre by brambles and branches. The pain where I was bitten by the black widow spider and where I was burnt with the red hot metal was killing me so I didn't really feel the extra cuts I was getting. I looked down at my index finger of my right hand. There were two red dots where the spider had bitten me and they were getting very red and swollen now.

The woods were getting thinner; I came out onto a fairly small country road with only a couple of houses in between fields and woods. I realised that I needed a vehicle otherwise I would never get away quickly enough. As I walked past one of these houses to my right I could see a car on the drive with all its doors and boot open. The owner I guess had been hoovering and cleaning the car. It was a good car for me to take; it was a silver Ford Mondeo. The sort of car people would never look twice at. I could see the back door of the house was open.

I walked up to the back door. As I walked past the Mondeo I checked the ignition barrel to see if the keys had been left in it. They hadn't. Damn, I was going to have to go into the house and see if I could find them.

I moved up closer towards the back door as silently as I could and that was when it happened. The poison from the spider started affecting me. It happened just like Mann said it would, only worse. I felt a massive pain in my stomach and it just made me drop to the floor in agony. Next I felt like all the muscles in my body had tensed up, then one by one, all my muscles began cramping and the spasms began. I looked down at my arm and there were muscles and tendons visible that I didn't know I had. I began convulsing on the floor and I screamed out loud in pain. I couldn't help it.

I then became aware of a man in his late 50's maybe with grey hair come running up to me. I could hear him talking to me. Asking what the matter was and then saying he was going to ring for an ambulance. I tried to say "no" but I couldn't, my jaw muscles were convulsing too much to speak. It was starting to become hard to breathe. The man had gone into his house.

I couldn't stay here but I was in a terrible state. I started dragging myself along the ground, past the garage at the end of the drive and into a hedge just behind it. Here I stopped. I started fitting again and convulsing. I was out of sight from the man now but I was not very far away.

I could hear him come out again.

He shouted, "Hello? There is an ambulance on the way, where are you?" I could hear him running up and down his drive looking for me. I had to get away from here. I tried to control my breathing which was still laboured, I started breathing in through my nose and out through my mouth to try and regain some form of physical control. After a few minutes my breathing returned to normal and the cramps in my muscles died down although my body was aching now all over.

I could move again now. I heard a vehicle pull up outside the house. Maybe it was the ambulance; I lay as still as possible and listened. I could hear the man speaking to the driver of the vehicle.

"He was here 5 minutes ago but when I came out again, he was gone, he looked in a right state and was having a fit."

I then heard another voice speaking but it was harder to hear. "Thanks for calling us, we'll have a drive around and look for him. We may have to call police as well to help us."

Then I heard the man's voice again, "Ok thanks for coming."

I heard the distinctive noise of a V8 ambulance engine driving off and I could hear the man walking back up his drive and closing his door.

I stayed where I was and began considering my next move. After about ten minutes, I heard the door open again and footsteps going to the Ford Mondeo. The door opened and closed, the engine fired up and after idling for a minute or two, the Mondeo drove off. Then there was silence.

I moved from under the hedge and had a look around the house. I tried the back door which was locked. I went back to the garage. There was a window in the side of it and I could see another car parked in there. I didn't want to take it but I would have to if I could find the keys. It was a black Lamborghini Diablo and was clearly the pride and joy of the man that only wanted to help me.

I went back to the house and had a look at the back windows. There was a rectangular hinged section slightly ajar at the top of the kitchen window. I could fit through this so I climbed up on the window sill and squeezed through.

I couldn't see any keys in the kitchen after a quick search and so I walked further into the house. I entered what was obviously a study and opened the desk drawer. There they were, a set of keys with a picture of a raging bull on them, the keys for the Lamborghini. I took the keys which also had what was hopefully the garage door key on them. I took a piece of paper from a pad and wrote a note…

> "*I am ever so sorry for taking your car. I have no choice as I am in a desperate situation. I promise I will look after your car while it is in my care and it will be returned to you. If any wear and tear is caused as a result of me taking it, Wessex Constabulary will reimburse you… Please contact Sergeant Lee Storker at Southmouth Police Station who will be aware of this.*"

I took from the man's desk, a piece of paper and one of his cheaper looking pens as I would need these.

Before I left the house, I had a look in his wardrobe. I needed something to wear as my t-shirt was ripped open. I found a medium size short sleeve shirt that fitted me ok so I put it on and then I left the house through the route I had entered.

I approached the garage, thinking to myself that the Lamborghini was an awful car for me to take, firstly it was someone's pride and joy, secondly I would stand out like a sore thumb and the car is so loud with its huge V12 engine I would be heard a mile away before I got to where I was going. Fast though, very fast so I doubted PSD would have anything that would keep up with me if I was spotted.

I opened the garage with the key and walked to the driver's door of the Diablo. The door of the car opens upwards and then you slide in. I got in and inserted the key in the ignition, turned it, vroom. The engine roared to life. It is difficult to describe how amazing a V12 Lamborghini engine sounds like unless you have heard it for yourself. These cars have nearly 500bhp so need to be treated with a lot of respect. I had a plan and a destination in mind and I hoped there was enough fuel in the car to get me there. I would try and drive conservatively as this car would use a lot of that.

I pulled out of the garage and drove slowly out of the drive. This car was certainly not going to make me go unnoticed, even with a light foot on the throttle it was howling down the road and each time I changed gear or lifted off the throttle there was a crackling and popping noise from the four exhaust pipes that sounded like a mini thunderstorm. Any other time I would have loved this but right now the Mondeo would have been a much better car for my needs.

18

The plan

It is an old wives' tale that the Lamborghini Diablo is a hard car to drive. In fact it's easy. For those who know their cars, it just feels a bit like a Lotus Elise with a great big huge engine instead of a four pot. It is quite a nimble car despite its width and size.

I managed to get on some A roads and saw a signpost telling me Crawley was 1 mile north. This was good news. My intended destination was closer than I realised, Gosport in Hampshire. I had a plan and it involved the use of a boat and I knew of a boat in the marina there that I would be able to use to execute my plan.

I phoned Louise as I was driving; it was great to hear her voice again.

"Hello?" she answered as she picked up the phone. She sounded more upbeat than the last time but still very quiet compared to her normal self.

"Hello Louise its Jack. Are you ok?" I said.

"Jack!" Louise's voice came to life "I'm better to hear your voice. Where are you? What's going on? Mollie is constantly asking when her daddy is coming home."

"I have got things in process and I reckon the odds are getting better now but I still have a lot to do to end this mess. How're you feeling?" I asked.

Louise replied, "Not so great actually Jack, I'm really worrying about you. I just got back from an antenatal appointment and my blood pressure is quite high. The midwife told me that if it doesn't go down again soon there is a risk I could get pre eclampsia."

Shit. Now I was really worried. I had read about pre eclampsia and I knew that it can be a life threatening condition for mother and baby.

"Louise, you must get to the doctors again tomorrow and every day just to get your blood pressure monitored," I said.

"Jack, when will all this be over? We just want you back," said Louise as she broke down crying.

I struggled to contain my own tears, "Hopefully as soon as possible my love. I have a plan that I am hoping will work. I have to go now but I will call again as soon as I can I promise, bye for now. I love you."

Louise replied, "Love you Jack."

I ended the call and cried to myself. I just couldn't help it; this was just the most unforgiving emotional rollercoaster I had ever encountered and I couldn't bear my family suffering too.

Next I called my solicitor. I had to be very careful how I said this as PSD would hear everything. My solicitor picked up the phone.

"It's Lucas. Are you free to talk?"

My solicitor replied, "Yes I can speak."

"Look right," I said to him. I paused before I continued. "I will meet you there on the anniversary of our first meeting. If I am not there, leave and come back in 24 hours. Do you follow me?"

To the right of my solicitor's desk he had a picture painting of a sailing boat going around the Needles which are some white rocks that stick out of the western side of the Isle of Wight with a lighthouse to prevent boats and ships from colliding with them. The anniversary of our first meeting was the 13th September at 0830 hours, conveniently only two days' time. My solicitor replied, "Yes I fully understand. Goodbye."

Then the phone went dead. Hopefully PSD wouldn't know what or where we were referring to and we would be able to have a covert meeting in the Solent where no one would be looking for me. I then threw the phone out of the window.

It took just under two hours to drive to Gosport as I took A roads rather than the motorway to avoid unwanted attention. I parked the car right in front of the Police Station.

I locked the car and posted the keys through the letter box at the side of the Police Station. It would be pretty obvious what car the keys belonged to and it would have been circulated as stolen by now I would have imagined.

Gosport is an old port right opposite Portsmouth and an old friend of mine I hadn't seen in a while kept a Sealine motor boat in the marina here. I knew where the keys for the boat were hidden and he had given me permission to use it whenever I wanted.

I walked straight to the marina and made my way down to the mooring for the boat I was looking for, there it was. Looking slightly 90's and out of date compared with more modern power boats, but a very impressive vessel nevertheless. I remember when my friend had new, more powerful engines installed. I knew it was fast. I hoped he wouldn't mind me taking his boat for a few hours. I found the keys, and switched on the electrics so I could see how much fuel was onboard, not much but I reckoned it was enough to get to the Needles and back.

It wouldn't take long to get to the Needles and I had just over one day to kill before setting out. The boat had two cabins, fore and aft and a full kitchen galley and was a very comfortable place to stay so I took full advantage of this and helped myself to the food in the well stocked fridge and cupboards and recuperated as much as I could while I waited for the big day.

19

The meeting

Thursday 13th September 2007 0600 hours

I didn't sleep much last night. My mind was on a million things at once, but mostly worrying about Louise and our unborn baby. I was also worried that I might not succeed in what I had to do but I couldn't think like that, I had to succeed and I would do anything to win this.

My meeting with my solicitor in the Solent where it joins the English Channel was set for 0830 hours. Still two and a half hours away but I wasn't sure how long it would take to get there so I fired up the boat's diesel engines, released it from it's moorings and slowly but surely manoeuvred the vessel out of the marina and into the main shipping channel between Portsmouth and Gosport.

As soon as I got into the waters of the Solent, I opened the throttles of the boat up to about 70% power to get some speed up. The waters were a bit rough today but it was an easy drive around the north coast of the Isle of Wight to the Needles.

I had spent Wednesday trying to rest listening to the clanking of boat masts in the wind. I wasn't worried too much about PSD knowing I was in the area after the Lamborghini was found as I couldn't imagine them coming into the marina and searching every boat. They would need separate search warrants for each boat but then again these people were hardly playing by the rules. I had just kept my head down below deck. There were lots of boats moored up here. Why would they think I was in a boat anyway?

I had time to think whilst driving the boat, jumping over the occasional wave as the spray went over my head when it landed back in the water, it made me wish that things were different and I had Louise and Mollie with me now out for a trip to the Isle of Wight. That wasn't the current reality though.

I slowed as I got closer to the Needles so that I arrived at the rendezvous at exactly 0825 hours when I dropped the anchor. There was no sign of any other boat but I was 5 minutes early. I made sure I stayed slightly north of the Needles as I remembered from the past that the water is very choppy where the Solent joins the English Channel.

I could see in the distance the shape of another motor

boat; I pulled out a pair of binoculars from behind the helm and looked through them. Yes, there he was right on time and 100% reliable as usual, my solicitor. He was driving a very new and purposeful looking Sunseeker motor boat. I found myself breaking into a smile as my confidence was beginning to grow that I was starting to win this fight now. All I had to do was tell him where Connor's post mortem report was and then I was on the final leg to getting the PSD cronies locked up and clearing my name.

My solicitor slowed down as he got closer and then as he was only a few feet away, he tossed a mooring rope over to me which I caught, I then pulled in his boat to mine and when the fenders on the side of the boat were sandwiched in between the two boats I tied the rope on to my boat.

My Solicitor jumped across with a big smile on his face. "You look like you have gone 11 rounds with Mike Tyson," he said as he shook my hand, "Where is our evidence?" he said.

I told him exactly where I had stashed Connor's post mortem report.

"Excellent," said my solicitor. "I will go there personally to retrieve it."

He had some news for me …

"Mr Lucas, I have informally met with your Sergeant, Lee Storker and he has some news for us. Inspector Mann had responsibility for the custody centre at the time of Connor's death. Connor had asked for medication for his heart condition which he had to take. No one got the medication for him because Inspector Mann had neglected to inform the duty nurse."

Ah, that would account for why Mann would want me fitted up for Connors death but, "Why are Burton and Link in on it, though?" said my solicitor speaking my thoughts out loud.

I replied, "Well Link is dead now anyway."

My solicitor shot me a concerned look.

"Self defence," I said as I shrugged my shoulders.

"Maybe they owed Mann a favour or maybe he had something on them if they didn't help him," said my solicitor. "Look you will have to give me full details of everything that's happened when this is all under control and we can meet in a more relaxed formal manner again. Link's death will have to be well justified but I am sure it was."

We were just about to wrap up our meeting and head our separate ways when I heard the distant sound of an outboard motor not very far away. I looked through my binoculars and could see a Rigid Inflatable Boat with four men in it travelling very fast towards us. The most concerning observation I had made however was that all four men were armed and right on the bow of the boat was a man pointing and aiming a Heckler & Koch G36 automatic rifle right at us.

"Shit," I said, "they're onto us. The boat is four up, all armed. We've got to get out of here now."

I quickly raised the anchor and fired up the engines while my solicitor untied his boat from mine so we could get away. I shoved the throttles right up to the top and the diesel engines roared into action as the bow of the boat went up and the back went down.

I wasn't sure how fast the RIB (Rigid Inflatable Boat) would be but I knew I would get at least 30 odd knots out of my boat. I was gathering speed when I heard a dull 'crack, crack' behind us. Then a split second later 'bang, bang' as what I could only assume were rounds from one of their weapons hitting into the hull of my boat. "Get down below deck!" I shouted to my solicitor. He did so.

I didn't know the range of the G36 rifles the men in the RIB were carrying but I had a pretty good idea that even if my boat was faster than theirs which was doubtful, it would take a long time to get out of the range of their weapons. Even so, I imagined it would be difficult to aim and fire a gun from a RIB bouncing up and down on the waves.

I decided running away wouldn't get us anywhere.

I pulled the throttles right back down to minimum power, there was a fast response as the nose of the boat dipped back down and the wake behind the boat overtook it and came over the back. Once I was happy we were at the right speed, I threw the steering strong port (left) turning the boat right around 180 degrees into the path of the RIB. The two boats were now nose to nose at a distance. Then I threw the throttles up to full power again. This brought the nose up and shielded us from any rounds coming from them. The only problem was now I couldn't quite see where the RIB was, I had to guess.

The RIB suddenly came out to my right; it is a far more manoeuvrable boat than the 40 foot motor vessel I was driving. I saw the occupants all lifting up their rifles except the driver and I saw flashes from their muzzles. I was completely exposed standing up at the helm so I just ducked and threw myself to the deck. 'Bang, bang, bang, bang, bang, smash' rounds hammered through the side windows of the boat and into the driving controls smashing dials and sending sparks flying. The impacting rounds suddenly ceased. I guessed they were manoeuvring the RIB in a position to board our boat and so we were temporarily out of their firing line.

I jumped up again to the controls and pulled the boat into a sweeping starboard (right) turn towards the mainland. I hoped that the time it would take the RIB to get up to speed again would put a good gap between us.

I looked behind and could see the RIB gaining ground; it must have had very powerful engines.

Again I could hear the sound of the G36 rifles firing at us and occasionally a round would whack into the boat somewhere. They were getting closer and now rounds were pouring in around the helm. I ducked down to the floor again. I left the boat driving itself on full throttle. I stayed where I was.

I could hear the RIB getting closer. They had stopped firing and I could now hear the RIB alongside us on the starboard side. They were trying to board our boat. I stood up and could see three of them about to jump onto our boat. I yanked the steering hard right into the side of the RIB. This caused the RIB to tip sideways and at least two of them fell into the water.

I looked behind and I could see the RIB slowing and turning to pick up its crew.

Now was the time to act. I pulled the throttles right down to minimum again and cut power, spun the boat round 180 degrees and slammed the throttles open again just like the first manoeuvre I did.

This time we were closer to the RIB so they had less time to react. They were in the middle of a slow turn and as such, had to gain speed before they could start any quick manoeuvres again.

"I've got you now," I said to myself.

I lined our boat up with where I thought the RIB would be once its speed was up and focused hard on the point. There was no way the RIB could get out of my way this time. I held a course with the RIB slightly to my starboard side so I could see its position clearly.

I closed the gap at about 20 knots. The RIB disappeared from my view as the bow of the boat hid the RIB. They hadn't got away and were floundering in the water.

There was an almighty bang as I drove our boat straight into the RIB. I was jolted forward and into the boats dashboard. I felt our boat lift right up and then crash down again on something hard. They were out of the game now.

My solicitors head popped up out of the hatch below deck.

"Deadly force again Mr Lucas? You do like to make sure I earn my money don't you?"

I smiled, "It's well deserved but it doesn't look like you do too bad out of it with boats like that one you turned up in," I replied.

My solicitor responded, "Yes, talking of which would you mind taking me back to my boat. I'm probably as much in danger as you now."

"No problem," I replied "how are you going to get to Keele services?"

"Leave it to me Mr Lucas I will get the evidence," said my solicitor confidently.

Then very suddenly and unexpectedly a man swung up from the side of the boat. I recognised this clown. He was a PSD Sergeant that used to work at Southmouth Police Station before he went to PSD to 'further his career'. He had a reputation for being very underhand in interview. A friend of mine once had to suffer a 5 hour interview with him that could have been completed in half an hour. His name was Andrew Crabel and he was the epitome of the PSD double standards arse hole.

Crabel lifted up his rifle into the aim position and there was nothing I could do, I was too far away to try and physically stop him. I just gritted my teeth and waited for the bullets to tear through me when I suddenly heard a noise like an arrow being fired, and then a loud thud as a harpoon went straight through Crabel's chest, stopping before it came out the other side of him. I looked down and there was my solicitor, just poking out of the hatch with an empty harpoon gun in his hand. I quickly ran over to Crabel and pushed him over the side while he was still dying. The last I saw of him was his shocked face as he disappeared into the wake of our boat. He had dropped his rifle on the deck of the boat. I picked it up and put the safety catch on. This could be useful.

"Looks like I'm not the only member of the deadly force club today, eh?" I said to my solicitor with a smile.

"Found it with a whole load of diving equipment down below," said my solicitor shrugging his shoulders.

I dropped my solicitor back off at his boat. We shook hands, "Good luck again Mr Lucas, hopefully we will meet again very soon," he said smiling.

I replied "Good luck to you too, please be careful."

"Oh, one more thing I nearly forgot," said my solicitor. He handed me a mobile phone. "I will call you on this when everything is put in place. PSD don't know about this phone or the other one I will call you on."

I turned the boat around and made a heading for the River Hamble on the mainland.

20

Bad news

If you follow the River Hamble all the way to the end you eventually get to a dead end in so far as the navigable river is concerned just before a place called Botley which is a small village.

I intended to get a train from Botley out of the area so I could try to lie low until my solicitor was back in contact.

I was pleased in one way as I felt that things were underway but I also felt like I had no control now and I had to rely on someone else. At least there was someone else on my side that was actively helping.

I didn't really feel like a police officer anymore. I had been told from other colleagues who had been put through PSD investigations that this is often how they feel. You kind of lose your sense of identity. Even though you know you are in the right and PSD are trying to twist everything around to look like you are in the wrong, you feel like the whole police organisation is closing ranks against you and all the investigations do is reinforce the reality that life is not fair and it doesn't pay to be the one of the good guys. It seems unbelievable that the organisation employs such nasty dishonest people to investigate police officers just to allow them to climb the promotion ladder.

I anchored the boat and took its little rubber dinghy tender out to the shore after I left my friend a note and borrowed a wrist watch that had been left in the boat...

"Mate, sorry about the state of your boat but it saved my life. My employer will pay to get it all fixed as it is their fault it's in this state. PS: Borrowed your watch. I'll get it back to you."

I looked at the phone my solicitor had given me and I thought about calling Louise. I hesitated, PSD would then discover the number of this phone but then I had a brain wave. I could call her dad on his mobile. I would be very surprised if that was being monitored.

I phoned Roy, Louise's dad but he gave me shocking news.

"Jack, we thought you were dead what's going on? Louise isn't here; she went with Mollie to the police station. They said you were dead and they needed her to come to the hospital with them to identify your body."

Fuck! "I'm not dead, I'm perfectly alive. Who was it that called Louise?" I replied.

"Some Inspector called Mann I think?" said Roy.

Shit, shit, shit, shit, shit...

"Listen," I said, "this is really important. Can you phone Louise and find out from her what's going on. Tell her to come home and that I am alive. I will call you back in 5 minutes." Then I hung up.

This must have been the longest 5 minutes of my life. I called Roy back... "Jack, her phone is off, could be because they are in the hospital."

I replied, "They are not in any hospital. Inspector Mann is not a good person. He has been trying to kill me. I can't explain now but could you phone Southmouth police station and tell Sergeant Lee Storker everything you have told me. Tell him I am alive and all about Louise and Mollie. Tell him Inspector Mann is trying to kill me and I think he is using Louise and Mollie to get to me. Lee Storker is a good guy and we can trust him."

Roy replied, "Oh my God! What are you saying? Are they in danger?"

"Yes," I replied, "but please contact Lee Storker."

"Ok Jack, will do that straight away. What are you going to do?" said Roy.

I replied, "I'm going to try and find Louise and Mollie and get them to safety. I will call you back in one hour for an update."

How was I going to find Louise and Mollie? Where had that evil bastard Mann taken them to? One thing was absolutely for sure, he wouldn't have taken them to the hospital.

I decided to head for the last place it was known Louise and Mollie had gone, Southmouth police station.

21

On the offensive

I caught a train at Botley station and headed for Southmouth, Wessex. I had put the late Sergeant Crabel's G36 rifle in a sports bag after folding up the collapsible stock of the weapon.

They had Louise and Mollie and I was absolutely furious. If the gloves were off before, well now I was doing the mental equivalent of putting on knuckle dusters.

I sat restlessly on the train to Southmouth now and I felt I had all the justification in the world to actively find Mann and kill him.

The carriage was busy with people but not full. I had managed to find some seating with nobody immediately beside or in front of me although there were a few people further down the carriage. It would have been an uneventful journey but for a typical 'customer' of my normal line of work.

At one of the train's stops an extremely dishevelled man aged approximately in his mid 40's entered my carriage. He had a 2 litre bottle of cheap cider and he absolutely reeked of booze and body odour. There were plenty of free seats but rather than sit down somewhere on his own, he sat right down next to an old lady who appeared to be with her two grandchildren and then let rip the most enormous belch I had ever heard. The children who were boys aged around 8 and 10 years old clearly looked worried. The old lady obviously wasn't scared to speak her mind and said, "You disgusting man, there are other seats, please sit somewhere else."

"Fuck off granny breath!" said the dishevelled man.

Great that's all I need. I wanted to keep a low profile and not draw attention to myself but I couldn't let this scum bag get away with this behaviour. I hoped he would move and nothing else would happen.

The old lady stood up and said to her two grandchildren, "Come on, let's move somewhere else." She took the two children by the hand and then sat down on the seats immediately next to me.

The dishevelled man got up and sat down next to the old lady again. On sitting down this time he let out another enormous belch that made his last seem tame. He looked over at me and said, "What're you looking at, prick?"

He then opened up his bottle of cider and held it out to one of the two little boys with the old lady. "Swig of special brew?" he said with a horrible cackle of laughter.

The boy reeled back in fright as the man took a swig spilling some of it down his front.

Enough was enough. I had to keep a low profile but I wasn't going to let this toe rag continue his harassment of these innocent people.

I opened up the sliding window next to my seat and then I walked over to the man. He was looking at me with a look of worry now – he probably wasn't used to people actually coming to him. I snatched his bottle of cider out of his hand, walked to the open window near my seat and threw it out.

"Rob me of my booze will you, you cunt," he spat at me with a look of real hatred.

I had dealt with his sort a thousand times before and I knew there was now a good chance he would try and get violent with me. I wasn't going to give him the opportunity. I leant down and grabbed him around the throat with my hand pulling his windpipe right out with my fingers. He was choking to breathe.

I turned around to the old lady and said, "Get into

another carriage, I won't let him bother you all again."

The old lady took the boys and left. I let go of the man's throat and said, "Sit still, shut up and don't you dare harass anyone else."

He just looked at me and nodded his head. Normally I would have arrested him for that even if I was off duty. I hated people like him, but current circumstances didn't really allow that so I just kept a close eye on him until, at the next stop the man got off the train.

As soon as he got off onto the platform he turned around and started shouting, "Fucking prick, fucking wanker, I'll have you next time I see you, I'll fucking cut you up."

He was looking at me through the window and waving his fingers around at me.

Where is the British Transport Police when you need them?

I realised that 55 minutes had passed since I had last spoken to Roy. I waited another 5 minutes and then called him.

The phone was answered on the first ring. "Hello Jack?"

"Yes," I replied.

"I spoke to Lee Storker earlier. He said he wants to meet you in the location where you nicked Connor at nine o'clock tonight," said Roy.

"Brilliant news. I will update you when I can but I need to be careful how much I use this phone," I said to Roy.

"No problem," said Roy. "I hope they are ok."

He was starting to sound seriously worried now.

"Me too Roy, it's killing me, speak soon."

I hung up.

Sergeant Lee Storker was a good bloke, a copper you could rely on and there are certainly not very many of those in today's 'modern police force'. I had every faith that he was not part of this crazy situation and that he would do whatever was in his power to assist me. I had to put my faith in Lee.

I arrived at Southmouth Central train station at 1800 hours. I now had three hours to kill whilst I waited for my meeting with Lee. I had to be very careful. I would be recognised by any police officer or criminal around here as I had worked in the area for so long. Luckily my beard was coming on and that would change the general shape of my face. I also kept my sunglasses on whilst the sun was still up.

I headed straight for the shops so that I was one among many for the time being, less chance of being spotted in the crowds. I pretended to shop for things, picking things up in shops and examining them as if I was thinking of buying them. I was completely lost in thought and worry about what they might be doing to my family and how they were right now. It had to be one of the worst feelings in the world. I felt so helpless. But I was determined I would find them and sort out Mann. Doing this for nearly three hours was really painful. Each minute seemed to take a whole hour to pass.

At just after 2000 hours, I made my way to the park where I had arrested Connor right at the start of all this. The sun had gone down but there was still a bit of light left, and it wasn't fully dark yet. I walked around the outside of the park checking for anything suspicious or out of place, basically anything that might indicate to me that this was a trap. Nothing seemed unusual. I then made my way out of the park and into the multi storey car park that overlooked the park. I climbed towards the top floor via the stairwell which stank of stale urine. I hoped the causes of the smell would not be there: the local No Fixed Abode heroin users, people like Kevin Fletcher who I was cooped up next door to when I was arrested and other such undesirables. They often slept in the stairwells or begged for money in them to spend on their next 'score' of heroin which is all they lived for. They would beg, rob, burgle and steal from anyone they could to get their next heroin 'score'. The stairwells were empty thank God. They would probably recognise me if they saw me, even with a beard. Once on the top floor, I took up a position near the wall and there I watched and waited. I could see the exact location where I took Connor to the ground and I expected to see Lee right there at 2100 hours.

2030 hours, no sign of Lee, as to be expected.

2045 hours and still no sign, again to be expected, Lee was as professional as he was reliable.

2100 hours on the dot and Lee walked into view. He was dressed in civilian clothing and I saw him look down at his watch. There was no one with him. I looked around the wider area and still could see nothing that would raise my suspicions that he was being followed.

I went down the stairs of the car park and made for Lee's location. I entered the park and walked towards Lee.

Lee saw me coming, he smiled and held out his hand which I took and shook, "All right mate?" he said.

We then continued walking and at the same time spoke. "Thanks for this," I said. "Did you see Louise and Mollie when they came in?"

"Yep," Lee said. "I saw them both come into the front

office. I spoke to Louise and she told me that you were dead. I couldn't believe it. No one has seen or heard from you in ages and the management won't tell us a thing about what is going on with you, I spoke to Louise's dad as you know. Louise and Mollie went into Inspector Mann's office and then he took them off in a van somewhere. I guessed it was to the hospital but from what I have heard from her dad obviously not! What the hell is going on Jack?"

I gave Lee a summarised version of events so far and I asked if he could help me. Lee's response was, "I'm a police officer because I want to do the just and right thing. I trust you Jack, you wouldn't lie to me about this sort of thing. I will do whatever I can to help you. We need to find where Mann has taken your family and I have an idea of where that might be."

I took great comfort in the fact that Lee had said "our side" not "your side." He was making me sure that I knew that he would back me up no matter what.

Lee told me that he was aware that Mann belonged to some sort of social club that owned a large mansion in the countryside outskirts of Southmouth. The building was mostly left unoccupied except when this social club had functions on. Lee thought it was a good bet that, that is where he would have taken my family.

Lee also told me that he had found a detention log sheet

in the confidential bin in custody that had recorded Connor had asked for medication for his heart, and this is how he found out the information he had passed onto my solicitor.

We made a plan to head to the place. There were only two of us and we had to expect an army of heavies on top of Mann and maybe even the swollen jawed Burton.

The odds were not good against us. I thanked Lee for his assistance but told him that I would prefer it if he took a support role rather than come in with me and risk his life. Initially Lee would not have any of it.

"No mate, I'm coming in with you. You won't have any chance on your own," he said.

I replied, "The only thing that will change with two of us is that me and you will get hurt rather than just me and in the laws of odds I shouldn't be alive now anyway."

I showed Lee the G36 rifle the late Sergeant Crabel had left me and told him to take it and be ready to support me with deadly force if necessary. Lee was an ex member of the Wessex Firearms Support Unit and knew what to do with the weapon if it was required. My instruction to Lee was to maintain observation on the house before and after I entered and to force an entry with his weapon if he suspected that I was compromised in any way. I took Lee's mobile number and told him I would call him on it if I needed assistance and that I would send an empty text to him every ten minutes. If I failed to text on time it meant that I was compromised and he should again, make a forced entry with weapon if I failed to text back on schedule.

We got to the building at just before 2200 hours. We had driven up there in one of the unmarked CID Ford Fiestas. Lee had taken it before meeting me.

What an unusual building. The gates at the front of the building read, 'Wessex Masonic Headquarters' – Some social club. I don't know much about the Freemasons but I do know that there is not supposed to be any association with the Freemasons and the police service, at least not one that the police would want to publicly admit to.

We could see that on one side of the building there was a kind of annexe to the main part of the building and there were lights on. There appeared to be silhouettes of people behind the blinds. We were still about a hundred yards away though and would have to get a closer look.

Lee took on his skipper role and suggested that we split and check out a different side of the building each. He suggested that he would check the lit room with the silhouettes and the rest of that side whilst I scouted around the other side of the building. What we were looking for were points of entry, preferably ones that could be entered quietly and covertly, security systems that might compromise us, any sign of the number of people in the building, exit points that we could use to escape from once we had hopefully rescued Louise and Mollie and also to try and get as much of a picture of the internal layout as possible which was going to have to be educated guess work on the external features and clues that we could see.

We agreed to meet up again at a specified rendezvous point in fifteen minutes time. We were not trained Special Forces soldiers, we were police officers and what we were doing now with just two of us was well outside our comfort zone, but what had been in my comfort zone since I had arrested Mitchell Connor though?

I scouted around the east side of the building as stealthily as I could keeping to the outskirts of the perimeter fence which was only four feet high. There was plenty of shrubbery and trees surrounding the building to keep me hidden from view.

There was an entrance at the very front of the building on its south side that would be the main door. There were four large windows on the ground floor, two either side of the front door. South east of the front door was a double garage and there was a very small outbuilding near this that looked as though it would probably be some sort of lock up for garden tools or something similar. I could see a padlock on it.

There was a car park which was empty.

The building had three floors.

On the east side of the building there were several windows of the same style as the south side of the building with a small back door right at the very corner. I could see one of the windows near the door was slightly ajar. They were the old fashioned style of window that is like an upturned rectangle in shape that slides up from the bottom – a sash window. There was no sign of life and there were no lights on this side of the building. I could see what looked like alarm boxes on the side of the building but I couldn't tell if these were fake boxes designed to put off burglars or real boxes that worked.

I moved around to the north side of the building and checked my watch; I needed to be back with Lee at our rendezvous point in 6 minutes. On this side of the building was a large back garden with a patio. I could see there was security lighting here and there were French windows that led onto the patio area from the north east corner. There were lots of windows on this side and everything looked dark inside. No lights were on and again, there was no sign of life. I couldn't see the annexe area from here but Lee would be covering that.

I made my way back to our rendezvous point and Lee was there waiting for me.

Lee went first. "No sign of life at all apart from the annexe area. There are three people in there. I got close enough to stick my ear to a window. One sounds like Mann and a woman and a child. It's got to be your family and him."

I felt absolute seething anger course through my body. How dare he take my family. He really would pay for this. I told Lee what I had seen.

We established that the best and only viable point of covert entry was the window I had spotted on the east side of the building. Lee was going to stay on the west side of the building listening at the window to hear what was going on in case I needed his backup.

I would climb through the window and make my way quietly through the building to the annexe where Mann was holding Louise and Mollie.

22

Making entry

I made my way once again to the east side of the building where I saw the open window. I climbed quietly over the fence and made my way to the window.

I stopped underneath the window and just sat there and listened for about three minutes. There was not a noise inside; you would have heard a pin drop. There was not quite enough room for me to get through the open window so I got my hands underneath and pulled the window up higher as quietly as I could. Unfortunately the window was old and would not cooperate with my wish for quietness, it screeched up on its runners. Shit! I stopped again and listened. This time I waited about six minutes before I moved again – no noise. Either no one had heard it or they were just waiting for me to come inside.

I sent a text message to Lee, 'In' I typed. To let him know I had made entry and was ok at the moment but that the job was now on.

I went in through the window. I was in an empty room with carpeted floor that led to another doorway. I went through the doorway being very careful how I stepped, making sure my feet made minimal noise as they went down. This led into a room with a drinks bar running along the side of it. The shutters on the bar were down. There were a number of plaques along the top of the bar, some were military charities and in pride of place there it was – the Wessex Constabulary plaque. Don't let anyone ever tell you there is no Freemason influence in the police force.

I moved quietly through this room to the door at the other end. Fortunately all the internal doors seemed to be open, almost tunnelling me to my destination. This doorway led into a corridor that had several closed doors running along it left and right, about 20 feet from my position was a small number of stairs leading up towards where the annexe area would be. I walked towards them. The walls all seemed decorated with pictures of Freemasons; there was a big wooden board with names of lots of people running down it, a glass cabinet full of strange looking objects of unknown use on display.

I was getting closer to the annexe. I climbed the stairs and there it was, an open door with light streaming out. I could hear Mann's voice taunting Mollie and Louise. I could hear Mollie crying and Louise trying to calm her down and all the while, Mann's voice could be heard calling them 'cry babies' and 'don't worry, soon it will all be over and you will all be dead'.

I'd heard enough… I stormed into the room running at full pelt, kicking the door out of my way and burst in ready to ring Mann's neck with my bare hands…

There was no one in the room. What were three silhouettes from the outside were three shop dummies, the sort that wear clothes in Debenhams with a spotlight behind them which was clearly positioned to make the silhouettes we had seen from outside.

I heard Mann's voice addressing me to my right. I turned and I was looking at a laptop screen on a table.

"Well now Jack I see you have found my little trap I set for you."

I looked at the screen and there was Inspector Mann standing with Inspector Burton of PSD and sitting on two chairs in front of him were Louise and Mollie. They were both gagged and tied down, I could see the fear in their eyes. Mann then walked around to the front of them and pointed a Taser gun at Louise's tummy, the bump that our unborn baby Jenson was nestled in and he then said, "Jack. You are going to give me the location of the report I desire or I will shoot Louise in her stomach. Her and your baby will not survive and poor little Mollie here will have to witness the whole thing; all you have to do is give me what I want. Shortly my friends will find you and take you to me."

Then the screen went blank and the laptop powered down.

I felt sick from the bottom of my stomach. I had never felt so helpless and emotional in my life. That twisted evil Mann had my family and there was nothing I could do about it.

Two doors suddenly opened up at the far side of the room that I had not noticed and six heavies all came out holding baseball bats.

I couldn't take all this lot on. They moved towards me, one running behind me to close the door so I couldn't escape. I recognised Dave from my last torture session. He said, "You fucking little shit. Before we take you we are going to rough you up a bit, ain't that right boys?"

As he said the last bit he turned around to his colleagues and made a little laughing noise. They all laughed back. Dave then pulled his baseball bat back and swung it towards me. I jumped back and it missed me. Dave laughed again. I felt rough hands behind me pushing me towards him. Dave swung the bat again at the same moment as I was pushed forwards and it connected heavily with my left arm. The force of the blow sent me straight to the floor. I could feel severe pain in my left arm and chest. Dave came rushing towards me as if he was going to kick me in the head like Mann did when I was last caught but it was at that moment that there was the most almighty crashing noise of broken glass and the sound of an automatic rifle blatting out rounds of lead … bang, bang … bang, bang … bang, bang… bang, bang… bang, bang, bang, bang, bang, bang.

I lifted my head up, my ears were ringing and there was smoke in the air and silence. There was Lee squatting down this side of a window with glass all around him, the barrel of his G36 rifle was smoking slightly and he still had the gun in the aim position at a figure who was crouched into a ball in the corner of the room. The rest of the heavies, including Dave were dead, their bodies scattered all over the floor.

23

Last man standing

I ran over and grabbed the heavy by his t-shirt and threw him against the wall. "Where is my family? Where has Mann got them? Tell me now or we will kill you too!" I was shouting at the top of my voice. I was angrier than I have ever remembered being in my life. I punched him on the back of his head. It was needless but I was overcome with emotion after what I had witnessed on the laptop screen.

"I'll take you to the place," the man said desperately. "Just please don't hurt me."

I replied, "Who are you lot? All muscles and show but when you are cornered you all fall to bits. Who do you work for?"

He replied, "We work for a firm called Underground Security we got a contract with the police."

I turned to Lee who by now had dropped his G36 rifle

on the floor, "How come you didn't shoot this one?" I said.

Lee just looked straight faced at me and said, "Ran out of bullets."

We questioned the man, whose name was Alex, on the location Louise and Mollie had been taken to. It transpired from what Alex said that they were being held in an old disused chicken farm just outside of Wessex. Alex told us that as well as Inspector Mann, there was another female police officer there – this must be Burton and also another officer who Alex seemed to think was the boss of Inspectors Mann and Burton. I was starting to realise that this went a lot deeper than just a handful of bent PSD officers for the boss of Mann and Burton was Detective Superintendent Carl Jones. Jones was the second in charge of Wessex PSD and I knew from past experience of communication with him regarding his unfair treatment of one of my colleagues that he was a complete arsehole and I knew that he held grudges. He didn't like me and I didn't like him and I made sure he knew it. If he was part of this then I would take great pleasure in causing him a lot of pain.

We tied Alex's hands behind his back with some rope we found in a store room in the building and placed him in the rear of our CID Fiesta, then secured him further with seatbelts. I sat in the back of the car with him while Lee drove.

Alex directed us to the area where the old chicken farm was. It was the perfect location for a group of bent PSD officers to get up to no good. It was set back in woodland with a very long, twisty dirt road that was covered in potholes. It was the sort of place noone would know was there and there was nothing around it for miles.

Alex had given us a good idea of the layout of the chicken farm. I drew a plan of it based on what he had told us. There were three main buildings... The building on the west side had a large door for vehicles to drop off and collect poultry. Connected to this via a single passage with doors was a smaller building with several offices along its northern wall. It was in one of these offices that Louise and Mollie were being held under lock and key – Alex told us that the office was the one on the far right of the room. This would be the eastern most office. This long room with offices is connected via another small corridor with doors to the incinerators which must have been used to dispose of dead chickens and waste when it was operational. There are three incinerators and one of them is still working. The incinerators are connected together in a line from north to south; the most southerly incinerator has a small door on its side. Alex could not say if this door would be locked or not but he said the wood it was made of was very rotten. There was only one floor and there were skylights in the roof of the office building. The hostile occupants were Mann, Burton, one other bent police officer and two more of his colleagues from Underground Security. He said most of his team were at the Freemasons lodge to make sure they had enough manpower to take me.

So it was 5 versus 2 if Alex was telling the truth but he didn't strike me as being paid enough or loyal enough to lie. We had the element of surprise on our side if not the numbers. They would think that I was only one and they would probably assume that I was under control by the Underground Security goons.

Before we set about to attempt to rescue Louise and Mollie, we had to do something about Alex though. We drove him to a wooded area further east of the chicken farm and tied him to a tree using the rope we found at the Freemasons lodge. We gagged his mouth so he couldn't shout or make any noise, then we left to plan our rescue after promising Alex we would be back to release him once we had finished our business at the chicken house.

We drove back to the area of the chicken farm and parked the CID car off the road behind a tree so it was out of sight.

Armed with the makeshift map layout I had made of the chicken farm and its immediate surrounding area, we made our way through the trees towards it. As we got closer I noticed smoke coming up from behind the trees.

They must have the incinerator on for some reason.

I checked my watch, it was now 0330 hours. A good time to catch them by surprise but then again, they would be fairly alert waiting for the Underground Security goons to bring me back and by now they would be wondering what was taking them so long.

We came through some more trees and now I could see the building. I could see the outline of light through the main doorway. The place was exactly how Alex had described it. I could see the chimneys to my right which were the outlets for the three incinerators. Smoke was escaping from the one furthest to the north.

We debated what to do next and decided to follow the same plan as we had made at the last building. Lee scouted around the west side of the place whilst I scouted around the east side through to the north.

We rendezvoused as before but really we gained no further information about the place than we already had except that there were some closed windows on the north side. There was no indication as to numbers of people there from what we had both seen.

"Lee," I whispered. "I reckon our best point of entry will be the skylight closest to where Louise and Mollie's cell is. Then once we have them we can escape through the incinerators to the old wooden door which we could easily break down," as I said this, I held my makeshift map out in front of us indicating with my finger the entry and escape route.

Lee suggested an alternative; "Or we could use one of the external ladders on one of the incinerator chimneys and then shimmy down the inside using our backs and our feet to lower us down like we do in rock climbing. The chimney diameter looks just about right for that. If we use a skylight it's a long drop to the ground and we are likely to compromise our rescue and ourselves doing that."

So we decided on our method of entry, we would take the incinerator route and hope that we could gain entry through the disused incinerator door from the chamber at the bottom of the chimney.

24

Into the hen den

It was a tricky climb up the ladder of the chimney trying to stay quiet as whilst the ladder was strong enough to support our weight climbing one at a time, some of the bolts where it was connected to the old chimney were a bit loose and rusty and would occasionally make a little squeaking noise.

I went first and the brief was that as soon as Lee saw me disappear at the top of the ladder, he would begin his climb up whilst I shimmied down the inside of the chimney.

I got to the top of the ladder. The chimney was approximately 30 feet high but from up here it looked pretty scary. It was quite a delicate process transferring from the ladder to the opening of the chimney and the ladder felt very precarious at the top.

I grabbed the outside of the chimney with both of my

hands and slowly lowered my body into the hole, and then I pushed my feet out until they were against the other side of the chimney. My back was firmly against the opposing side and as a result I was kind of lodged into the chimney. From this position, I slowly lowered my feet a small amount down and then I slid my back down to the same level. It was a very deliberate, slow movement and it took some time before I reached the bottom of the chimney.

When I got to the bottom I was surrounded by cobwebs and dust, I could see the entrance to the incinerator chamber was open. It was a small gap but if we slid through on our fronts we would be able to squeeze through.

I looked up and could see that Lee was silhouetted against the early morning sky at the top. I gave a low 'click, click' noise with my tongue against the roof of my mouth which was my signal to him that he was clear to descend and that we had a way in.

Lee descended using the same technique as I did and joined me. We squeezed ourselves in turn through the small opening and came out into an area close to the old wooden door that we intended to use as our escape route. I walked up to it and tested it to see if it would open or not. It was a bit sticky, sticking to weeds on the ground the other side of it but I could tell it would open with some applied force. I wasn't going to do that yet though, we were on stealth mode.

I turned around and could see that the room narrowed into a small opening where there was another of the incinerators – luckily we didn't go down that chimney as the door for that was locked and bolted this side. We would have had to go back up again and find a different way in.

We went through this room endeavouring to remain as quiet as possible. This led us to the working and currently operating incinerator. We could feel the heat from it and there was a veritable furnace of flames burning away in there, so it must have been hundreds of degree's C behind the closed door. It was very hot in this room.

Now it was crunch time – I knew from Alex and the layout that I had drawn up from his information that Louise and Mollie were being held in a locked office which was the first office on the right after going through the short corridor that led from this incinerator room.

We moved as silently as possible along this corridor. I couldn't see anyone in the room beyond but in the distance I could hear the sound of a child screaming. It sounded like Mollie and it appeared to be coming from the room that was next to the office room.

I reached the door that Alex said Louise and Mollie were being held in. It was locked shut by a bolt – that was all, just a bolt on the outside of the door. I looked through a small window on the door and Louise was right at the window looking scared out of her wits. I unbolted and opened the door, Louise fell into my arms crying.

"How…" she said, I stopped her.

"I love you. We are going to get out of here. Where is Mollie and are you ok?"

Louise replied, "That fucking bastard Inspector bloke has got Mollie. I'm going to kill him."

Fucking bastard; the law of the land would say he should be tried in court for this but I fully intended to kill him. Summary justice and I had already decided his sentence – death by my bare hands.

"Lee here will take you to safety, please follow him. I'm going to go and get Mollie, don't worry," I said. "I love you."

I kissed Louise and she said, "Please, get Mollie. I don't know what I will do if she is hurt."

With that, Lee escorted Louise back the way we had come past the incinerators and to the old wooden door.

I made my way to the doorway of the next room where

I could now hear Mollie crying. I could hear Mann's voice, "Afraid of spiders are we?"

Oh no! He's not doing that to Mollie, the poison would probably kill her, she is only six.

I peered slowly through a gap in the door frame and this is what I saw …

Mollie was on a chair in front of a table facing away from me. There was a heavy from Underground Security holding onto her by her shoulders. On the table in front of her was a glass case with a spider in it just like the one Mann used on me the last time we met. Mann was leering over the table at Mollie with that horrible evil smile of his. He was clearly taking pleasure out of torturing Mollie. It seemed he was just taunting Mollie with it at the moment. I could see Burton sat down over a desk at the far end of the room writing up some sort of paperwork and there he was, Carl Jones second in charge of Wessex PSD himself walking around near Burton with a mobile phone stuck to his ear. He seemed to be leaving a message for someone and appeared quite irate and angry. Maybe he was still waiting to hear back from Dave.

I heard Mann say to Mollie, "I am going to put your dad's hand in this hole here and the spider will bite him."

Mollie was crying her eyes out.

Then Mann said, "Then I will put your mummy's hand in and it will bite her and then I will put your hand in. The poison will kill you because you are only very little."

Mann was definitely a dead man walking.

I looked around me. I was looking for something to use as a weapon. There was a table not far away from me between me and Mollie. On this table were a number of tools that were probably used to gain access to the disused chicken house. One of the tools was a crow bar.

I broke my cover and ran for the crow bar, picked it up without breaking my run and carried on for the Underground Security heavy holding onto Mollies shoulders. He turned around towards me just as I was within one footstep from him. I caught a glimpse of Mann's face. He had a look of sheer terror. In the next split second I swung the crow bar with the pointed bit facing outwards with every ounce of power and speed I had straight into the side of the head of the heavy holding onto Mollie... Crunch! It embedded itself into the side of his head and he went down to the floor with bright red blood oozing quickly out of the wound. The crow bar was still stuck in his head.

Mann tried to run away. Not this time. I covered the ground to Mann and grabbed him around his neck. He was a tall man and I was quite short so he was naturally pulled backwards by my hold and I took him straight to the floor. I pinned him to the ground and held his right hand in what is known as a goose neck lock. I was pulling his hand hard in on itself towards his forearm causing him pain. I looked over at Mollie and said, "Mollie, run that way and keep running until you find a door. You will find mummy and a friend of ours there. Go now."

Mollie ran off as instructed.

I looked around. Jones and Burton were nowhere to be seen. They had obviously taken the opportunity to make good their escape. The Underground Security heavy was now surrounded in a pool of blood.

Mann started struggling and trying to resist. I punched him in the side of his head.

"Stay still scum!" I said. "You are going to pay for this; I'm going to fucking kill you."

I lifted Mann up and threw him head first into a wall. He bounced off and landed on the floor. He stood up again and this time threw a punch at me. It was a rubbish punch and it missed. Clearly no one had ever shown him how to fight properly. I blasted him with a combination of fast, hard punches. I was in an absolute rage now and I had never known anger like this existed. I kept punching him until he was barely able to talk coherently. He was trying to say something but I couldn't quite work out what it was.

"Ha ... hate..." he was trying to say.

I picked him up and put him in an arm lock and walked him to the incinerator that was burning. Mann continued struggling along the way but I had him firmly under control like a cat holding its kitten by the scruff of its neck. I opened the door and the heat spewed out sending a blast of hot air at us. Mann seemed to realise what was going on and suddenly picked up another burst of energy as he tried to wriggle from my grip. I hit him with an elbow strike to the side of his head to stun him and then I changed my arm lock into a wrist lock so that I held him at the end of his twisted arm which was now in a straight line from my hands to his body, I then slammed my fist down as hard as I could just above his elbow as I pulled up with my left hand. This snapped his arm and broke the bone. Mann howled in pain. I used his broken arm to manoeuvre him in front of the open incinerator. Then he said something a bit more coherent.

"I hate you Jack, I hate y..." his voice was sharply cut off as I hurled him with all my might into the burning incinerator... Woosh!

Mann went up in flames and I slammed the door shut." Good riddance.

I thought I could hear the sound of a helicopter outside flying away.

I ran back to the door that was our escape route to look for Louise, Mollie and Lee. I could see it was open and broken down now. I stepped through…

25

Reunited

Louise, Mollie and Lee were waiting outside the building for me.

Mollie and Louise ran over to me and I grabbed them both in my arms, lifting up Mollie to our level. We all cried.

"I love you all," I said.

Then I rubbed Louise's bump where Jenson was and she looked at me and said, "I think he's ok."

Mollie then asked, "Dad did you kill them?"

I just changed the subject straight away.

"Are you ok?" I said.

"Did they do anything to either of you?"

Louise replied. "No, nothing physical, anyway, just lots

of threats and I thought we were all going to die." Louise burst into tears again and I held her tight to me.

Lee came up to me, "Burton and Jones got away," he said. "They ran out of the main door and around the building; I would have gone after them but I wanted to make sure Louise and Mollie were ok, then the next thing a helicopter took off from where they had run to. Must have been them."

At least Louise, Mollie and Jenson were safe.

I looked at the chimney connected to the incinerator where I threw Mann; the smoke appeared darker than before. I don't know if it was my imagination or not but I thought I saw the shape of Mann's face just very briefly in the smoke, then it changed colour again and became lighter.

So far, Link was dead, Crabel was dead, Mann was dead and a number of Underground Security monkeys were also dead. I wanted Burton and Jones to go through the criminal justice system (such as it is). Someone had to live with what they had done. What better place for bent PSD scum bags like those two than prison.

We took Louise and Mollie to hospital. I wanted to get them both checked over. Louise's blood pressure was still high and it was recommended that she stay in overnight

I stayed overnight in the hospital with Louise and Mollie. There was no way I could leave them after what we had been through. Louise was given a private room to herself in the hospital. I just wanted Louise to start to feel better and for our baby boy inside her to be safe and to be born healthy and hopefully not affected by events that had taken place. I was also seriously concerned about the psychological effects of what Louise and especially Mollie as a six year old had been through.

The next day Louise was given the all clear to return home. Home was not a safe place for them now; there was no way they could return there with Jones, Burton and God knows who else out to get me.

I phoned Roy.

"Roy it's Jack. Louise and Mollie are safe."

"Oh thank God for that!" said Roy. "Where were they? Are they hurt?"

"They have been through the mill a bit to say the least but they are both ok now – Louise has been checked out in hospital and they say she is ok. I need you to come and get them both. They are still not safe at home, so can you come and take them somewhere safe? Sorry I didn't call before, I got a bit caught up in things," I replied.

"That's ok Jack, I'm just pleased they are safe now. It's such a relief! I'll get in the car right now and pick them up. I'll take them somewhere safe and I won't take my eyes off of them. What about you?" asked Roy.

"I still have some work to do to catch the people responsible and put an end to this all," I replied.

Roy countered, "But surely the authorities can deal with them now?"

"I can't trust the authorities, these people are supposed to be the police of the police. I can't trust anyone at the moment. I must see this through myself." After further discussion, Roy conceded what I had to do.

I stayed with Louise and Mollie until Roy turned up. I promised Louise that I would be in contact whenever I could on her dad's phone. I gave Louise and Mollie one last hug and lots kisses. We all cried. How dare those corrupt PSD bastards put us through all of this?

I forgot about Alex, the heavy we tied to the tree until the next day. I had broken my promise to him, oh well. I'm sure someone would find him at some point.

Whilst I was also now concerned about the consequences of my actions in killing Link and Mann,

I felt absolutely certain that I could justify my actions in the circumstances. My task now was to hunt down Burton and Jones and bring them to justice and in doing so, clear my good name.

26

On the trail of criminals

Saturday 15th September 2007 1000 hours

I met again with Lee. We had arranged to meet again at the same place as last time, where I originally arrested Connor.

It didn't sound like Lee had got much sleep. He had gone back to Southmouth nick and did as much research on Jones and Burton as he could. He didn't come up with much, the duties system would not allow him to access their personal details like address, telephone number etc. Lee could find nothing at all on Jones but after speaking to people that knew Burton he uncovered that she was homosexual and had a relationship with a married female police officer which had caused much controversy at the time – surely she shouldn't have been allowed a job in PSD with the knowledge that she could be so deceitful. She was clearly a dishonest person with ill morals in the first place but then, maybe that is why PSD employed her.

Working for PSD is similar in a way to selling your soul to the devil, if indeed you had one in the first place.

I told Lee about the 'special detention centre' in the Lake District. Lee didn't live far away and had an internet connection so we went to his house to do some research on Google.

We scoured Google for quite some time and the only thing that sounded like a good possible match for the 'special detention centre' was a disused World War 2 research station based in a similar location to where I estimated the 'special detention centre' was. This old research station was mostly underground and had been sold to a private firm in the 1960's whose name was not disclosed. No further information was available on this location but at least we had an address for a place that might be what we were looking for – I thought it a good bet that Jones and Burton had gone to ground there.

I told Lee that I could easily find the location that I dumped Link's car from Lancaster but I might have trouble retracing my steps from there. From memory I drove the BMW M3 which is a very fast car flat out for at least half an hour with lots of twists and turns along the way. We brought up Google Earth and looking at the road network north from Lancaster I was able to retrace my route from Lancaster to where I dumped the car. From here we had to make estimations from the location I dumped the car to the location of the WW2 research station... It fit together quite nicely; the old research station was in the right heading and approximately the right sort of distance away to be a very strong possibility. We decided to go there then all I would have to do is look at the outside of the place and it would confirm whether or not this was the 'special detention centre' where I had been a temporary resident.

27

Back where I started

It had taken us over six hours to drive up past Lancaster into the Lake District from Southmouth in the little CID Fiesta that we were still using.

From the place I dumped Link's car to the old research station took a lot longer than it took me to do the journey the other way around but then we were just plodding down the road this time in a diesel Fiesta at a much more sedate pace.

We pulled up one mile short of the research station and continued the rest of the journey on foot across country. As soon as we were in sight of the place my spirits were lifted – it was definitely the same 'special detention centre' that I had been brought to that seemed all that time ago.

We found a good spot to observe the place unseen.

There were fewer cars in the car park than when I was here last. I could see three cars and a large size minibus. The security hut was unmanned and I could not see any sign of security personnel in the car park. The barrier was lowered and some fencing had also been pulled across it. They were clearly not expecting many people to come and go from the establishment at the moment.

I had more time today to take things in around the hill. The perimeter fence was still just as high as I remembered it was before, about 20 feet with curled barbed wire around the top to stop people climbing over. We circled the hill and noticed that on the other side of the hill, the land dropped steeply and about another fifty feet or so at the bottom of the hill was a wide concrete platform poking out of a wide entrance. Lee had brought a pair of binoculars along so I took these and had a look through them.

The concrete area appeared to have lights on the end that were unlit. I couldn't quite work out what this was for. It almost looked like the very end of an aircraft runway. Then about sixty feet from this entrance was another perimeter fence that was slightly lower than the rest of the fencing. Beyond the fencing was a wide lake with a mountain on its far side.

The establishment was a nice secure location, but how were we going to get in?

Lee had brought along his 'burglars' kit bag' which contained amongst various other useful items, some bolt cutters. We took the cutters to a part of the fencing near the front and cut a hole big enough for us both to climb through.

We were through the perimeter fencing and now had to find a way into the 'special detention centre'. The obvious option was the door I escaped out of before, but that would probably be locked and I didn't have the key anymore for it. I didn't expect to be trying to break back in again.

From our observations the other side of the perimeter fence and from what we had seen so far within the fencing, there was no other obvious route into the place apart from the door I had used to escape through previously. Neither of us could see any other options.

We made our way to the barred door and tried it. It was not locked and just swung open when pushed. The place was very quiet. There were no lights on and absolutely no sign of life inside at all.

Lee pulled out a torch and switched it on. We walked over to where I marinated the three Underground Security heavies with CS by the desk. It looked like a reception type desk and it had a computer terminal, several television monitors and next to these, a bank of switches. I hit the switch labelled 'Lights: floor 1'. One by one fluorescent lights lit up above us and down the corridor leading to where I had my original interview. Next I switched on the computer terminal which booted up and then, whilst waiting for the computer to boot up, I spotted a switch labelled, 'cctv monitors'. I pressed this and the bank of television monitors sparked up into life. I looked back at the computer monitor. It was asking for a user log on and password ID. That was no good then...

The CCTV monitors were displaying various other parts of the place that I had not seen on my last visit. They were all still images with nothing moving. Interestingly though it appeared that other parts of the establishment had lights on. One monitor showed a picture of two Cessna light aircraft in what looked like a hangar – so it is a runway at the other side of the hill! It must be mostly underground for the aircraft to reach take off speed and then they pull up on the concrete at the end. I was pondering this as I saw movement ... I studied the camera hard. I could see Carl Jones opening a door to one of the planes and placing a large bag inside it.

"Look at this Lee," I said.

Lee came over and took a look. "Got you, you fuckers," said Lee.

Then in another CCTV monitor I saw Burton. She was

talking to a group of four Underground Security gorillas and they were all nodding their heads to whatever it was she was saying to them. They appeared to have a number of bags next to them as if they were going to load up the other plane… and then in another camera I saw two more of the Underground Security heavies stood by what looked like a lift door which they appeared to be guarding.

Lee tapped me on the shoulder, "Check this out Jack," he said.

I turned around and Lee was pointing at a map of the hill which was on the wall behind me. It showed a cut away picture detailing where we were and it mapped out how to get around to the various different floors and rooms of the place. It was quite an extensive layout inside, but there was one main lift that went down to the hangar area, and failing that there was a staircase down too. It occurred to me the lift must be where the heavies were guarding. We would take the staircase down.

To get to the staircase we had to go right past the room I was interviewed in, past my old cell and then all the way to the other end of the corridor where there was the main lift and the staircase alongside it. We had to descend past three floors to reach the hangar area. There were floors under this still and interestingly, a hall that had a water pool that led out to the lake behind the hill via an underwater tunnel. We would not have to go down that far.

We made our way along the corridor past my old cell; all the doors were open showing empty rooms. There was still no one in sight and no sounds at all. The lighting gave an eerie feeling to the place I had not noticed before, bright enough to see but dark enough to give the place a feeling of foreboding and malice. I found myself wondering what the place was used to research in the dark days of World War 2.

At the end of the corridor we ignored the lift and went straight to the stair well which was just through a set of double swing doors. We walked through the doors. The stairs were unlit. There was silence. The double doors squeaked slightly on their hinges as they closed then silence again.

A few seconds later the silence in the stairwell suddenly changed. I could hear a heavy panting breathing sound and fast, light footsteps moving quickly up the stairs below us coming in our direction…

A dark shape jumped out of the darkness at me, an open mouth snarled and I could briefly see the white of sharp animal teeth and drooling saliva; before I knew it, the mouth closed down on my right forearm. It felt like my arm was being crushed in a vice. Then the mouth of the animal, a big dog whose breed I couldn't identify in this light started pulling my arm left and right like it was trying to tear it off. All the while it was snarling angrily. I could feel my shoulder straining at its socket then I saw Lee moving swiftly towards the dog; there was a big thumping noise and the dog released its grip on me and made a little whining noise. Lee had kicked it hard in its ribs. I quickly got up. I didn't want to take any chances that the dog had been put off so I jumped on its back and grabbed its head in my hands holding my left hand around its jaws so it couldn't open them to bite and also so I had control of its head. Then I closed my right fist and hit it as hard as I could five or six times on the back of its head and neck then I yanked its head back as hard as I could. Crunch! If it wasn't dead from the strikes then it was definitely dead now. I had broken its neck. The dog dropped from my hands. My forearm was bleeding and felt an awful state.

I felt sad, I love dogs and the poor animal was only doing what it was taught to do. Still, better a dead dog than a dead Jack I thought.

Lee interrupted my grieving for the dead dog.

"You ok mate?" he said.

I pulled up the sleeve of my jacket and inspected my arm. It was bruised and there were puncture wounds where the dog's teeth had broken my skin. Blood was dripping from my arm.

"Just a scratch Sarge," I joked as I pulled off one of my socks to wrap around the wounds and stem the bleeding. Lee didn't look convinced.

"Come on, let's go and get them before they take off," said Lee as he led the way down the staircase.

28

Low flying

We descended the stairs quickly but were careful to keep our noise to a minimum. The stairs went down several small flights interspersed with landings.

I was hoping that there were no more dogs and also wondering how the hell we would arrest Jones and Burton with at least six of the heavies protecting them.

Almost in answer to this Lee patted my arm with his hand. I looked down and could see that Lee was holding a can of CS spray in his hand.

"I nearly forgot, here take this," he whispered.

Well that balanced the odds slightly more in our favour, but they were probably armed with far worse than CS spray – still, at least we could use the CS to disable the heavies for a limited time and I felt more prepared now.

We had no plan for what we would do when we got to

the runway area. We just didn't know exactly what we would be faced with. At the moment all we knew was that there were two bent PSD officers and at least six heavies. We had a basic knowledge of the layout of the floor – there was a hangar on one end and a runway that led to an exit from the hill at the other end. There were two light planes and at least one of them was being loaded up by Jones and Burton to depart. My guess was that they were cutting their losses now and making a run for it. They realised they had no chance of obtaining the evidence against them and they knew it was only a matter of time before the evidence was used to show the world who they really were.

In a way I had already won; on the assumption that my solicitor had successfully recovered the evidence that is. I could just easily turn around and wait for things to take their natural course and everything would be ok for me and the Lucas family. But there was no way on God's earth that I was going to let Jones and Burton get away. They had done too much to us and they were going to pay.

We passed a door with a sign over the top of the door frame that read, 'Test bays'. The sign was old and I guessed it was a fitting from the station's original purpose. We carried on past this door and we knew now that there were two more floors to pass, it was still dark but my eyes had adjusted to this and I could see a lot more clearly now than I could when we first entered the staircase.

We passed the other two floors. One had a nondescript door with no obvious indication as to where it led to, the other had no door at all and all I could see down it was a very long dark corridor which disappeared into the darkness.

Eventually we reached the door we were looking for. It even had a sign above the door frame like we saw before but this one simply read, 'Airfield'.

"This is it," whispered Lee, "ready?"

"Let's have a listen at the door first," I replied.

I wanted to be as prepared as possible. The door was simple and plain painted wood with a common type of handle. I could tell from the hinges that the door opened inwards towards us. I stuck my ear to the door. I heard what sounded like something metallic dropping to the floor and echoing, then the sound of a male voice cursing someone else. I dropped down to the bottom of the door as I could see light through the gap. Doing this I couldn't see properly but I could see shadows. There were two shadows either side of the door. One of the shadows moved. It was someone's feet. The person, I guessed one of the heavies, moved away. The other shadow remained but I saw it move slightly. Then after a few seconds the other shadow came back.

"There are at least two of them the other side of the door," I whispered to Lee. I took Lee further away from the door to enable us to speak more freely without being heard and discovered.

"We need to deal with these two as quickly and quietly as possible," I said.

"What's the plan?" asked Lee.

"You open the door; I'll go past you and grab the man on the left. I'll pull him back through the door and choke him out until he goes to sleep. You do likewise with the man on the right," I said.

Lee replied, "Ok, seems to be the safest way of doing it and we'll also take the number of bad guys down by two. What if we've got it wrong and there is more than just two behind the door?"

"Then I'll just draw the CS spray you gave me and marinate the lot of them," I said. "Remember, we need to be really quiet so whilst we are strangling them, keep one hand over their mouth so they can't scream."

Lee thought for a few seconds in silence before saying, "There is no other option, let's do it."

Lee took position on the door handle while I went down to the floor again to have another look and listen. The two shadows had not moved. I got back up again and took up position behind Lee ready to go through and grab the man on the left of the door. I patted Lee on his shoulder to let him know I was ready.

Lee opened the door and I didn't hesitate. I moved through and grabbed the man on the left with my left hand on his mouth and I simultaneously pulled my right forearm around his neck. I felt him tense up but I had taken him completely by surprise. I saw Lee move to my right and grab the other man. I dragged the man backwards and into the darkness behind the doorway. As I did so I pulled my forearm back on his neck with all my strength. I saw Lee do the same as he kicked the door closed with his foot. Lee was really struggling with his victim and while mine was trying to head but me with the back of his head, I moved my head to the side and pulled it in close to his head so he had no more room to head but and also to give me some extra leverage to pull my arm against. I kept pulling my forearm against his neck and the man was bucking like a bucking bronco trying to get free from my grip. I kept strangling and he kept trying to fight it until after a few more seconds I felt him go limp. I kept the pressure on for a few more seconds just to be sure and then I let him drop to the ground. He was unconscious. It was then I realised that Lee was still struggling with the other one. I quickly joined him and I could see that this other man was tucking his chin in tight to his chest so Lee couldn't get a proper choke hold on his neck. I punched the man hard in his ribs as a distraction strike. This was enough to put him off the battle of keeping his chin down and Lee managed to get a good hold on his neck. I helped by holding his hands down whilst Lee continued his choke. Eventually the man went to sleep. Lee was soaked in sweat and looked relieved the battle was over. Remarkably we hadn't made much noise but I imagined the door slamming shut might have drawn some attention.

I found a dark corner behind the last flight of stairs and we dragged the two heavies into it.

I heard a voice behind the door.

"Where're those two fuckin slackers? They were meant to be stood here at the door."

I heard another voice respond from some distance away but I couldn't hear what it said. The voice nearest the door seemed relatively satisfied with the response and his voice moved away from the door as he was walking away, "Fuckin idiots! Why do they have to go to the toilet with each other every time?"

The hangar area seemed to be where most of the activity was coming from. This area would be to our right as we went out of the door and this was the area we would need to head for. On the map that we had of the station, there was what looked like a small office high up on one of the walls midway down the runway. I imagined this would be a control room of some sort.

I suddenly heard the sound of a propeller engine start up. No way was I going to let them take off and get away...

"Come on," I said to Lee. "We can't let them get away." I pulled the door open and ran through with Lee following closely behind me.

I could see the Cessna lined up at the end of the runway. There were three people in it, the pilot, Burton who was sat next to him and Jones was sitting behind them. I didn't know if the plane was ready to take off or not but suddenly the noise and engine revs of the Cessna picked up and its wheels started moving slowly forwards. I looked around; I couldn't let these bastards get away from me. Then I saw what I was looking for, a large panel on the wall only five feet from me. There was a big green button and a big red button under the script, 'Main doors'.

I ran to the panel and slammed the bottom of my fist firmly on the red button. A siren started sounding and red lights all across the roof started flashing. I looked at the end of the runway and I could see two doors very slowly closing inwards. I looked at the Cessna and it was picking up speed. Clearly the pilot was still going to chance it and try and beat the closing doors. Then I saw a door open on the far side of the Cessna, a figure jumped out, rolled on the floor and stopped. It was Jones. I watched as Detective Superintendent Carl Jones, second in charge of Wessex PSD lifted up a pistol from a kneeling position, pointed it in our direction and then, bang, bang, bang, bang, started firing at us.

I ran as fast as I could towards my right. I could see a tractor type vehicle which I assumed was used for manoeuvring aircraft within the confines of the underground runway. I was going to use this as hard cover. I got behind it and dived behind its back wheel where I hoped the wheel axle would protect us from the bullets; us? Where was Lee?

My thoughts were interrupted; I heard a terrible crashing and ripping noise. I looked in the direction the noise had come from, the doors at the end of the runway. The Cessna had not made it. The wings had been ripped off and the remains of the fuselage were just the other side of the doors. At least Burton hadn't got away.

The firing from Jones's pistol had stopped. I could see four heavies congregating to my right. They didn't appear to be armed. I still didn't know where Lee was. It suddenly dawned on me that the fact Lee hadn't joined me and the firing had stopped was a very bad thing, "Oh no!" I exclaimed, I peered around the left of the tractors wheel and then I saw Lee. He was face down on the ground. There was a pool of blood flowing out of his head and there were more red holes in his body. Lee had made the ultimate sacrifice to help me, his mate. I was starting to feel the same rage inside me again as when I killed Mann. I had to keep it under control, I wouldn't survive here in that frame of mind, I had to have a very clear mind.

"Come on Lucas, get out from behind there. Your Sergeant is dead and it's all your fault," came the voice of Jones.

I hadn't come this far to surrender. Even if I wanted to it was quite clear he would not let me live after watching him kill Lee. I looked around me again. There was nothing behind me to assist and I could see that the heavies further away to my right were looking quite relaxed now they could see Jones apparently in control of the situation, pistol in hand. One of the heavies ran off towards the crashed plane that never managed to lift off, presumably to check the occupants were ok. I looked up into the cabin of the tractor. The keys had been left in it.

I climbed up into the cabin of the tractor and turned the key – I knew how to drive one of these from my days living in Hereford as one of my friend's dads who was a farmer had shown me how when I was a kid – the tractor started up, I looked around and I could see Jones approximately three feet from the rear of the vehicle. He raised his pistol again; I shoved the tractor into reverse and drove backwards towards him. Jones must have been just about to pull the trigger when his instinct for survival overruled his passion to kill me. He jumped out of the way. I swung the front of the tractor around so he was in front of me and engaged a forward gear. The time this took gave Jones time to run away from me towards a door under the office window high in the wall. I was gathering speed and was gaining on him now. Too late; he was through the door and there was no way the tractor would fit through. I stopped and then realised that the three remaining heavies were sprinting up towards me. I didn't have time to engage reverse and move the tractor. I had to fight.

The first heavy got to the door of the tractor cabin and flung it open. He had one hand holding onto the side of the cabin to pull himself up and the other hand was still holding onto the open cabin door. He was completely open and unready for the kick that connected right under his chin. The kick was not powerful enough to do much damage as I had executed it from a very awkward position, however it was powerful enough to knock him off the tractor and stun him. I jumped out of the cabin and before the heavy could pick himself up off the ground, I hit him straight in his temple at the side of his head as hard as I could with a downwards elbow strike using my weight and momentum going downwards to add to the power... smack! His head bounced off the floor, he was still conscious but very dazed looking. The other two came running up to me. I drew the CS spray Lee had given me earlier and squirted the nasty liquid out at the two men. One stopped dead in his tracks and dropped to the floor screaming, the other stopped running and looked slightly confused. He put his hand to his face as if to work out what it was he had been sprayed with, then he started blinking and held his arms out in front of him like a man who had just been blinded. CS affects different people in different ways. I then stepped towards the second heavy and threw a full power right cross straight to his chin... crack, he went down out for the count. I went over to the first heavy I sprayed with the intention of doing the same. He was still squirming around on the floor rubbing his eyes and screaming. I got up close and hit him full power with a right hook to his jaw... bang, he went down but he was still conscious – he certainly didn't have a glass jaw. I took him into a choke hold and strangled him unconscious.

By now the CS was affecting me again too, although not as bad as it had affected the two men I had sprayed as they had it directly into their eyes. I was just getting up from putting the man to sleep when the first heavy that attacked me in the tractor cabin was approaching me again. I had some CS spray left; I aimed it at his face and squirted him too. He went down in a ball of streaming water from his eyes and snot from his nose.

I ran up to him and booted him with a kick to his jaw. He was out.

I went over to Lee's body. His body was in a right state. He had been shot in the face and the round had come out the other side of his head, on top of that he had been shot several times in his body.

"Sorry mate," I said to his lifeless form, "thanks for saving my life and helping my family."

There was nothing I could do for Lee now.

At that moment the phone my solicitor had given me rang ...

29

Submerged

Saturday 15th September 2007 2245 hours

I answered the phone.

"Lucas, go ahead."

My solicitor's voice. "Hello Mr Lucas. I have our package and I am about to hand it over to someone who will help us. We need to meet to discuss the next steps. Can you make it to my office in the morning?"

I replied, "That's great news but I'm in a rather difficult position here. A lot has happened since we last met and I'm currently trying to detain Burton and Jones in the place where I was interviewed."

My solicitor's voice again, "Jones? Carl Jones the PSD deputy?" he sounded surprised.

"Yes," I responded, "it goes right to the top level at PSD.

I need to get going. Can you call me back in one hour?"

"No problem – please stay alive Mr Lucas," said my solicitor.

That was brilliant news about the evidence package. I had mixed feelings though. I felt sad and guilty about Lee being killed trying to help me. I was worried about Louise still with high blood pressure and the possibility of her getting pre eclampsia. It was time to focus on the job at hand though and turn my worry and sadness into positive energy to complete the job of nicking Jones and Burton then I could get back to my family and continue life.

Jones and Burton were going to get it and if I had to I would kill them as an alternative to arrest if there was no other choice.

The runway area seemed empty apart from the three unconscious heavies. I looked back towards the doors where the wrecked fuselage of the Cessna was now resting with its tail just inside the doors wedging them open. I ran over to it to have a closer look. It was empty. Burton and her pilot had got out – this meant I still had four hostile people to contend with, the pilot, the heavy that ran to the crashed Cessna, Burton and Jones. I was only interested in the PSD cronies although the other two would make things trickier.

I looked out of the doors. I didn't think that Burton and

the heavies would have gone that way. The fencing was very high outside with barbed wire around the top. The part where the fence was lower was also covered in barbed wire on the top and on the other side was the lake. They must have escaped through the same door as Jones went through whilst I was fighting their colleagues.

I made my way to the door and had a peak around the corner; I didn't want to run into an ambush. There was no one there, just a corridor that went straight for approximately twenty feet and then turned abruptly right. I couldn't see any further than this. I didn't know for sure where this corridor would lead but looking at the map I had of the station, it would probably lead to the hall underground. It was marked on the map as 'Underwater Research'. There was a tunnel in the hall that led out to the lake the other side. It struck me suddenly that they may be using this somehow as an alternative escape route. I wasn't going to let them get away from me.

I carefully rounded the corner and the corridor continued another ten feet forward before an abrupt left turn. At the corner was a small staircase going up. I edged to this junction. Now I had a choice. I could go up the stairs or round the corner. I guessed that the stairs went up to the office / control room that overlooked the runway as on my map I could see no other route back up the station than the lift or the stairs we had originally come down. I felt it extremely unlikely my targets would have gone that way as it was likely to be a dead end. Therefore I carried on around the corner. This took me to the start of a spiral staircase going downwards.

I studied the top of the staircase. It was not ideal as at any point there could be an ambush awaiting me and it was really obvious to them which way I would come from as there appeared to be no choice of route other than down the stair case. I noticed that on the wall just next to the top of the staircase was a venting system of some sort. I took out my map; I wanted to see if it was marked on my map and if it might be an alternative way down than the staircase. I studied my map when … whack! I felt something very hard and heavy hit the back of my head. I dropped to the floor and turned over on my back just in time to see Jones leaning over me with his pistol in his hand. He pulled the pistol hand back and threw it back down at me and before I knew it everything went black …

I had a splitting headache …

… I was waking up. Where was I? It was very light in here and appeared to be a big cavern with very bright lights all around the ceiling. I couldn't move; I looked around me and I could see that I was tied down with rope; I looked left and right, I was on something hard and metallic floating in a pool of water. I looked down at my feet; all I could see was a bit more of the surface I was tied to which ended in a slope and then went down to the water. The water went on for about forty feet before ending at the cavern wall. It dawned on me suddenly that I must be in the hall marked 'Underwater Research' on my map.

"Ah he has awoken," a voice came from behind me.

I heard two sets of footsteps and saw two people walking around me and into my view. Detective Superintendent Jones and Inspector Burton.

Burton spoke, "The Boss here has authorised the use of deadly force on you Jack."

Her jaw looked less swollen now so she was probably only just starting to become able to talk without pain again since I hit her with a perfect right hook the last time we were in this place.

Jones carried on, "You are tied to a submarine Lucas. This submarine is our transport out of here since you destroyed our aeroplane; you will be coming with us too. The only difference is we will be inside the submarine and you will be outside. I will enjoy watching you drown from the observation window."

I replied, "Well it seems I will die then. Before I die, tell me what this is all about. How come so many of you

PSD arseholes are involved? I understand Mann's motivation to cover up his mistake in custody, but why are you, Burton and the rest involved?"

Jones seemed to consider this. He rubbed his chin and looked thoughtful. "You are about to die," he said, "it won't harm now to tell you. Mann had information on some of us in PSD that he threatened to leak out if we didn't help him make you take the blame for Connor's death. This information would have led to criminal charges being brought upon us. Mann is dead now but it's rather too late for us to pretend none of this has ever happened, so you must die and we will disappear."

With that the two of them walked back around me the way they had come and I could hear their footsteps fading away.

I was tied down really tightly; there was no give in the ropes at all. I couldn't see how I could possibly escape what now seemed to be my inevitable fate: drowning tied to a submarine driven by PSD. What a way to go! Not what I had in mind. I had to work out how to get out of these ropes.

I looked down at the ropes. I could see one rope around my ankles, one around my waist and I could feel another piece of rope around my upper chest area which was also holding my arms down. I tried to sit up with all my strength to try and find some give in the top rope; I did the same with my feet. I heaved and heaved and heaved. Then I relaxed for one minute. I counted in my head, and then I heaved and heaved again for all I was worth. I relaxed again. I tested the rope by my feet for any slack. It was slightly slack now. I pushed up with my left foot while I tried to pull my right foot out of the rope – it was working. I pulled out my right foot, then with more slack I was easily able to pull out my left foot. I could feel the top rope around my chest was now not so tight but the rope around my waist was. I pulled my feet up close to my bum and pushed down with my feet while I tried hard to push my pelvis forward, straining at the rope. I followed the same pushing and then relaxing procedure I followed with the other bits of rope and eventually I had a little bit of slack. With this and using my feet to walk myself painfully and slowly down, I was able to slip the chest rope over my head.

Now I could sit up. I was just about to try and slide out of the waist rope with the assistance of my free hands when the submarine started up…. I could hear an engine running and the submarine started slowly moving forwards. I then became aware that the surface I was still tied to was getting lower and water was coming over the sides onto me. It was freezing and it made me take a gasp of air.

I was still tied to the submarine by the middle rope. I took a big gulp of air; the submarine went under with me tied to it.

30

Justice

For a few seconds all I could see and hear were bubbles around me. I felt panic take over me. I knew I could only hold my breath for a short period of time and I was still tied to the submarine with the middle rope. I felt for the rope with my hands and found it. I pushed the rope downwards whilst at the same time, trying desperately to squeeze out from under the rope. I was managing to squeeze out inch by inch. A few seconds later and I was free of the rope but I was desperate for air! I let go of the rope and all of a sudden part of the submarine seemed to hit me, it was the tower section where I imagined Jones and Burton had entered the vessel. I grabbed hold of what looked like some sort of aerial mast that was poking out of the top. I got a glimpse of a semi circular window that poked out of the front of the tower. I could see Jones at the window. He didn't look happy; he was after all, expecting to see me drown tied down to the deck of the submarine rather than out of his sight.

The aerial broke off from the submarine in my hands and I went further back down the submarine. I threw my hand out desperately trying to grab part of the submarine to stay with it and I managed to grab one of its tail fins at the back. I was right next to the propeller, holding onto a tail fin in one hand and the broken off aerial mast in my other. Strangely, although I was starting to feel light headed now, I was feeling a bit more relaxed holding my breath underwater. I had an idea … I rammed the aerial mast into the propeller; the aerial seemed to be made of fairly sturdy stuff so I hoped it would help stop or damage the propeller. The mast lodged in and the propeller pulled the rest of it in, nearly yanking my arm off in the process. The propeller stalled for a second then spun up again, then stalled one more time before coming to a stop. By now, I was feeling desperate to take a breath; it felt like I was on the verge of drowning.

The submarine wasn't going anywhere, as it had no propulsion now. I could hear a rasping sound and I could feel water pressure coming from above, I realised the submarine was surfacing! I could see light above me and it was getting lighter and lighter, I was barely holding onto my breath… splash! The submarine had surfaced and I breathed out and took in deep grateful lung fulls of fresh air. I looked around me and I could see that we were approximately twenty feet from the other side of the hill. I could even see part of the smashed up Cessna through the fencing. It was a brightly lit night with a full moon and not a cloud in the sky.

I pulled myself up onto the deck. My clothes were heavy with water which poured out of and off of me as I hauled myself out of the lake and onto the submarine. I felt weakened by the strain of holding onto the submarine as it was moving along. I stood up on the deck and had a look at the top surface of the submarine. There was a small hatchway at the rear of the tower. The submarine had lost its propulsion and wouldn't be able to go anywhere now until it was fixed. I was hoping that they had assumed I had drowned and it was a simple mechanical failure that had stopped the propeller.

Surely someone would have to come out of the door and investigate the propeller. I moved up to the port side of the tower and crouched down so no one would see me if they came out that way.

Sure enough, after 5 minutes or so the door opened up and a man came out. It was not Jones. It must be one of their hired thugs. He was wearing a wet suit and was carrying breathing apparatus. It was obviously his job to get into the water and have a look at the propeller. I watched in silence as the man lowered himself into the water. I heard a voice, Burton's voice in the doorway.

"Get it fixed asap and then get back in."

Then I heard the door close again but it hadn't been sealed it was just resting on the frame. I watched the man swim around to the back of the submarine and then I lowered myself onto my front and I crawled slowly and quietly to the rear of the submarine near to where the man was working at the propeller.

I could see him pulling bits of the aerial out of the propeller. He didn't know I was there and was focused fully on his task. I crawled back to the tower again and found part of the rope that had been used to tie me down. I found the knot and I undid it. I then carefully coiled the rope up and then slipped into the water on the port side of the boat. I ducked under the water with the rope and swam around out to the port side putting some distance between us, then when I estimated I was about ten feet out from the submarine I turned left. I could see the stern of the submarine and the fins that the man was wearing fixing the propeller under the water. I was behind him now. I surfaced to take a fresh breath and then I ducked down again with the rope held between my hands... I closed up on him. I was within one foot from him when I surfaced and pulled the rope tight around his neck. He struggled, I pulled harder. I pulled as hard as I could for what seemed like an age. It felt like I was getting cramps in my arms it was taking so long. I could cope with this though, I just switched my mind off from the pain, I had dealt with a lot of pain recently and this wasn't going to beat me. Eventually the man relaxed, he was either unconscious or dead. I took his chin in my hands and swam with him back to the port side of the submarine just as I had been taught how to rescue people from the water at Ashford Police Training School. I hoisted him and myself up on the port side of the tower where we were out of view. I looked down at the man.

Perfect; he was pretty much the same height and build as me and he even had a slight scruffy beard like I did at the moment. I stripped him of his diving gear and wet suit and put them on myself, I put the face mask down over my face and attached the breathing apparatus to my back with the mouth piece hanging loose. I left the man there on the deck of the boat and I made my way to the hatchway.

I went through the hatchway and down some steps. I made sure I left the door open. Burton was looking down at something on a laptop computer, I had a look at the screen and was horrified by what I saw, it was a series of photographs of police officers. There were even one or two there who I knew. I was there too and the title above the photographs was, 'PSD Prolific Priority Offenders'.

I always thought that PSD would have something like that – real police have presentation slides and photos of real criminals like burglars and robbers. PSD have replicated the same thing for police officers they want to persecute; unbelievable.

Burton didn't really look up from her work properly and said, "Is it all fixed Andy?"

I shook my head to indicate the answer to that was a negative.

"Well get back out there and sort it out!" she said.

I turned around, there was Jones right behind me, and he was looking over now at me.

"Just need to fire up the motor and test it," I said in a semi whisper to try and disguise my voice.

Jones looked at me with an odd look and said, "Something wrong with your voice?"

I replied by coughing to make it appear as if I had something wrong with my throat.

I sat down at the controls and found a red button. I didn't know what it did but I pressed it anyway, the engine sparked into life. I looked behind me and I could see the door was still open; good. I found what looked like a throttle lever in front of a kind of half steering wheel which must be the steering and diving controls for the submarine. I pushed the throttles full forward. Andy had obviously done a good job trying to fix the propeller. The submarine started moving forwards.

"What the hell are you doing you fool the door is still open!" shouted Jones. I pushed the steering controls full forward as I assumed this would make the submarine dive. The submarine started diving. Brilliant; Burton just stood up looking panicked. Jones ran for the door to try and close it.

"No fucking way you PSD shit head," I shouted. "This time you are going to drown."

I put the mouth piece of the breathing apparatus in my mouth as I grabbed Jones's legs and yanked him back down the ladder. He punched me in the face and knocked the mouth piece out. I punched him back much harder straight into his nose which exploded in a spray of blood.

Water started pouring down through the open door and down the steps into the submarine. It was filling quickly. I turned around to Burton and said, "I was going to nick you but it's easier to just kill you both."

I then grabbed Burton by her hair and shoved her head down into the filling water pool that was now at waist height.

"Drown you stupid bitch!" I shouted.

I recognised now that I was in a rage similar to when I killed Mann. I had never experienced this before but I guessed that this whole situation had changed me in some way.

The water level was rising; it was now at chest height. I put the mouth piece back in so I could breath oxygen from the tank on my back and swim out of the open door leaving Burton and Jones to drown but it was at that very moment that I felt something pulling me down from my legs. I went under and there was Jones with a little small tank of oxygen hanging from a face mask. In his hand was a long wicked looking diver's knife. I threw a punch at his solar plexus. It connected but it was no good, the water had taken the power out of the punch and it felt like I executed it in slow motion. It had no affect on him and in retaliation he lunged at me with the knife thrusting it forwards towards my gut. I moved to the side of the knife as I used my left palm striking his wrist to deflect the knife and the lunge missed. I was now in Jones's 3 O'clock position just to his right; Jones was still holding the knife out at full extension from his arm. Before he could recover from missing his strike I quickly took his wrist in my right hand. Whilst I did this, I positioned my left forearm under his arm but above his elbow joint and then I grabbed my right arm with my left hand. I then pushed down with my right hand and up with my left forearm – this pulled his elbow the wrong way on itself and is a position I know causes a lot of pain whoever is on the receiving end.

Jones dropped the knife. He had no choice. I grabbed

him by his head and shoved him into the floor of the submarine whilst I felt around for the knife with my other hand. I found it … I held the double edged knife in my right hand with the blade pointing down my arm rather than out of the top. I grabbed Jones by his hair and pulled him towards me, and as I did this I swiped forwards with the knife to his throat. I missed but from this position and with the knife held in the manner it was, all I had to do was pull the blade back the other way and this is what I did. The knife embedded itself in the side of Jones's neck. Blood came out of his neck and floated out into the water like red smoke. Jones was dying. It was time to leave the two bent PSD scum bags to their well deserved fate.

By now the entire interior of the submarine was completely full of water. I looked behind me to where I left Burton. Her eyes were wide open and lifeless, she was dead.

Jones's blood was now filling the submarine. I had obviously stuck the knife into his jugular, the main artery that carries blood to and from the brain. He must have been dead but I wanted to check. I swam through the red misty water until I found Jones. There was still blood coming from his neck but not as quickly as it was coming out before. Jones, like Burton had wide open lifeless eyes, and his mouth was open. He too was dead.

Job done.

I swam through the open hatchway and out of the small submarine. I looked behind me and could see it lying on the bed of the lake, a watery coffin for Inspector Burton and her boss, Detective Superintendent Carl Jones, the dead deputy head of Wessex PSD.

I realised I had done a favour for every decent Copper in Wessex Constabulary today.

I swam up and eventually I surfaced to the most beautiful night sky I had ever seen. There were millions of stars in the clear night sky above me and the moon was shining brightly on the lake. I swam for the shore near the hill.

I had done it; I had brought the rotten PSD apples to justice.

Epilogue

Thursday 1ˢᵗ November 2007 1400 hours

Louise and I were in Wessex Hospital Maternity Ward; earlier in the day I went with Louise to her week 39 antenatal appointment, her last one. We had assumed everything was fine as her blood pressure had gone down again following the aftermath of recent events. The midwife checked Louise's blood pressure and it was high again, this combined with some other symptoms meant that there was again, a risk of pre eclampsia and as a 'precautionary measure', the mid wife had told us to get to the Maternity Unit at Wessex Hospital immediately for Louise to be observed.

I told Louise on the way there, "I reckon by the time we are coming back together, we'll have Jenson with us." Louise and I were very nervous.

When we got to the hospital Louise was set up on a blood pressure monitor and before long her blood pressure went dangerously high. Louise was moved to another room which was clearly a delivery suite. I said to her that I thought they were going to start inducing labour. We were both excited by this and at the same time very nervous and anxious. Louise's blood pressure was very high at that moment.

The midwife came in, an older more experienced sort who seemed very calm and reassuring to us both; she was talking away to us when Louise suddenly said, "I think my waters have broken." Louise put her hands between her legs. It was blood. Then very suddenly, blood covered Louise's trousers and was all over the bed. The midwife pressed the nearby panic button and her cool casual demeanour vanished, she was looking panicky. Louise's trousers and underwear were pulled off and blood was gushing out.

"Oh for fuck's sake," I thought "Jenson is dead, please just save Louise. I couldn't carry on without her." I felt desperate but I didn't want to show my inside panic to Louise, I wanted to be reassuring to her as I knew she would be so worried. She had grown Jenson and cultivated him inside her all this time. We already loved him even though we hadn't met him yet. This was awful.

Lots of people rushed into the room, all asking Louise several questions at once until one of the doctors seemed to take control. I held Louise's hands so she knew I was there but I moved back to allow the medical professionals to get to her. A quick scan was made of Louise's tummy and I could see Jenson on the screen and I could see his heart beating – but slowly.

A decision was then quickly taken to take Louise into theatre. I followed along to be with Louise but I was stopped at the doors to the operating theatre and told I was not allowed. I shouted after Louise, "They are taking you into theatre. I love you." I was then taken back to the room by an elderly midwife and offered a cup of tea.

The midwife didn't really know what to say to me and I didn't know what to think. I was pretty certain Jenson wouldn't make it and I just now wanted Louise to live. I thought about how hard this was going to be for us to cope with.

I felt awful – worse than I have ever felt in my life. I just didn't know what to think and I felt it was very unfair for this to happen to us especially after everything we had been through.

The midwife went away for a while and I was left on my own.

After a few minutes she came back and told me, "Your boy is alive and ok, he is just being taken down to the Neonatal Ward to be checked over." I felt elation that Jenson was born but it was overshadowed with my worry for Louise.

"How is Louise? Is she ok?" I said.

"I don't know yet," the midwife replied.

I was panicking now. Why weren't they telling me? The midwife went away again.

After a few minutes she came back, "Yes she is ok but she is having a blood transfusion and will take a while to recover."

It transpired that Louise lost nearly a third of her body's blood in the space of minutes. Louise had a placental abruption. This means that the placenta in which Jenson had been living and supplied all his nutrition etc had actually come away from the inside of Louise's body. This was caused by the pre eclampsia it turned out she was suffering from.

Had we not been in the hospital, Louise and Jenson would be dead without doubt. We were so lucky!

Jenson was introduced to me on my own while Louise was still recovering – not ideal as I wanted us to meet our son together but Jenson would have had to wait a long time to see us both if we were to do that.

Eventually Jenson was taken to his mum and then a couple of hours later Louise was wheeled back in her bed to the room that I was waiting in. Louise looked absolutely beautiful holding our son who was suckling on her breast despite the fact she looked tired, white faced and puffy. I kissed them both.

Mollie was at school while all this was going on so I phoned Roy and he and Louise's mum Sandra picked Mollie up from school and came straight to the hospital.

I was so happy but at the same time, angry as I felt that this was caused through the stress Louise had to go through because of the process I was put through. The pregnancy was going fine until PSD started ruining things. Even just the fact I was investigated for a simple assault on Connor would have made Louise stressed let alone all the other shit we had to contend with.

In relation to all the recent events, my solicitor had forwarded the evidence to a contact he had in Interpol, an investigator in their Anti Corruption Unit. This officer was apparently already making an investigation into possible corruption in Wessex PSD and the first thing he did on receiving the evidence was shut down the whole PSD department suspending the lot of them from duty and passed their role to the IPCC (Independent Police Complaints Commission) while he conducted his investigation.

The Interpol Anti Corruption Unit that conducted the investigation concluded that the Wessex PSD was responsible for a lot of malpractice and many criminal offences were found to have been committed by lots of its Officers over the last two years. Many Officers from Wessex PSD were arrested and brought to justice including the head of Wessex PSD, Chief Superintendent Andrea Boylan.

Although the evidence had cleared me of the Manslaughter charge I still had to account for the people I had killed.

I had personally killed Caseworker Link, Inspector Mann, Inspector Burton, Detective Superintendent Jones, at least two heavies as the man called Andy who fixed the submarine propeller was found dead in the lake and a dog.

The only death out of that lot that I felt any remorse for was the dog.

The actual body count was much higher due to the group that Lee shot in the Freemasons HQ. Lee could obviously not account for these deaths as he was not here anymore but I would make sure that I would for him as his witness.

Of course my solicitor was also responsible for the death of PSD Sergeant Andrew Crabel. With me as a witness and my poor friend's boat seized as evidence it was deemed that my solicitor had acted in defence of me and himself and no action was taken against him.

Irrespective of my lack of remorse and no matter how justified my killings were, I would have to face murder charges for these deaths and that would mean that I would have to be remanded in custody until the cases had been fully heard. This would probably take years of extensive court proceedings and I wouldn't have much of a family life in the meantime.

The question was when would it all catch up with me? I knew it would at some point. I couldn't just pretend I didn't kill anyone.

The question was soon answered ...

Seven days later I arrived home from the hospital with Louise, Mollie and Jenson. We had been in the house for approximately five minutes and were just in the process of showing Jenson around his home when there was a knock on the door.

I answered the door to see two men in black suits. One of them held up a warrant card to me and said, "Jack Lucas?"

"Yes, that's me," I said.

He responded, "Mr Lucas, I am Detective Inspector Ross of the Independent Police Complaints Commission, no doubt you have been expecting us. You are under arrest on six accounts of murder …"

To be continued …?

Afterword

Q: What's the quickest way for a decent person to become a criminal?

A: Join the Police!

Right this very second as you read this, several police officers who are honest decent people who perform their jobs properly and diligently are being investigated by PSD. Lots of them are so stressed they don't know what to think about it all. Many of them are suffering a complete injustice which is totally out of proportion to any allegation made. Many of them are so stressed they are right this second contemplating suicide.

I have been there. I know.

They are being punished for doing the jobs they have been trained to do. They are being investigated for doing their duty.

When will this change?

When will the decent British Bobby be treated with dignity?

When will EVERY investigation on a police officer be fair, impartial and above all, professional.

If you are considering joining the police and reading this book has put you off, good. It is a taste of reality they don't tell you about when you join up.

Wear the uniform and your greatest enemy is not the criminals, it's the Professional Standards Department in your force. If you are a serving police officer yourself reading this, remember and heed my words. If you are a PSD officer reading this and you know that you fall into the bracket of 'malicious investigator', how the hell do you sleep at night?